The Secret Slipper

The Secret Slipper

Amanda Tero

The Secret Slipper

Published by Amanda Tero
Decatur, MS 39327

ISBN: 978-1-942931-23-2

Cover design by Amanda Tero
Images from
www.pixabay.com
Elizabeth Tate, SunKissed Photography
Used by permission.

Formatted by Amanda Tero

To Grandpa and Grandma Carpenter

You have always been cheering me on
and encouraging me in whatever hobbies
or businesses I put my hand to. I love you!

Prologue

Kiralyn Castle

Another grave. This time, a short one. Nes tossed the spade onto a patch of unturned earth and stood straight. Mayhap the plague would take him next and spare him from seeing body after body plunge from healthy to dead. He was old enough. His aching back provoked the reminder. He looked at the hole in front of him. He'd rather die himself than bury another child—let alone the lord's child.

Turning from the empty grave ready to receive its burden, Nes walked toward the castle, his footsteps slow. In a few hours, the blonde lass would be buried beside her mother—two fresh graves, waiting to welcome Lord Kiralyn home. Nes shuddered. At least he was not the one telling Lord Kiralyn. He only had to bury the child once the friar finished the service. Within time, the lord would move on and find another wife. Mayhap raise another family. His riches provided such luxury—unlike Nes, whose lot in life had never altered from when he was a lad.

Nes brushed his dirt-encrusted fingers on his breeches and stopped at the well. He drew a bucket of water and let its weight settle on the stone ledge. The yard was silent, like it had been for the past few days—as if people were afraid to breathe anymore.

Nes splashed water onto his face, letting the cool droplets run down his dry cheeks. If someone would hand him a passage out—whether by death or by journey—he would take it. Any place where he did not have to spend his days burying the losses from the plague.

He turned and looked at the castle behind him with a frown. Lord Kiralyn should be here, not out fighting war with some other vassal. He had money enough to send an army of trusted knights and stay behind himself, seeing to the needs of his own serfs here at his castle.

Laughter trickled down to the courtyard. Nes's frown deepened as he looked up at the windows of the castle. The days had been too long and sorrowful. Mirth shouldn't come from the castle for a long while. Especially not the morn after Ellia's death.

A blonde head bounced in front of the open window. Nes squinted as he looked harder at the window, rubbing a rough hand over his face. He was at the castle door before he realized he had left the well.

Though no royalty was around, Nes found himself glancing over his shoulder before entering. He hadn't been in the castle before, but something wasn't right—either his mind, or…

Things were as silent in the castle now as they had been in the yard. Nes hesitated before rushing up the corridor toward the window he had seen from below. The lass was still there, taking one uneven step after another. He brushed his forehead as he watched the limp.

"Child!" Sharp tones echoed through the passageway.

Nes slipped into the shadows as he recognized the voice as Ellia's nursemaid, Bioti. Hadn't he been told that Bioti ordered the grave? Chills crawled through his body as he saw the nursemaid lunge toward Ellia, jerking her away from the window.

"I told you to stay in the room."

"Mo-er." Ellia pointed in Nes's direction. He flattened himself against the wall and held his breath.

"Mother is dead. Now hush so we can leave."

When the nursery door slammed shut, Nes stepped forward. He looked out the window, the open grave in clear sight. If Ellia was alive, then whose grave had he been digging? And where was Bioti planning on taking her? He turned and opened the door that Bioti had entered.

Bioti spun around, her long skirts hiding the lass. "Nes!" Her slate-gray eyes hardened. "Shut the door."

He stepped into the room and pushed the door closed with his back. "Methinks you have some explainin' to do."

"Methinks not." Bioti stepped up to Nes, her young face smooth and unreadable.

"Whose grave be I digging?"

Bioti's mouth lowered into a frown. She reached into her russet kirtle and pulled out a pouch. She held it toward Nes, shaking it so that coins clanged against each other. "You are digging Ellia's grave."

"Nay, I am not." Nes looked from Bioti to the child, whose fingers had slipped into her mouth. "What be ye doing?" Or should he ask what she was planning on doing with the little lass?

Bioti straightened. "I see that as none of your concern." Her fingers clenched the pouch.

"If ye touch the lass—"

"Fool. I'm not going to kill Ellia." Bioti pressed the pouch into Nes's hand. "You need to dig a grave for me in the peasant's plot—convince the others that I died too. Bury something in it; it doesn't matter what."

Nes threw the pouch down and grabbed Bioti's shoulders. Surely the plague had made her mad. "Think calmly—"

"I have done nothing but think, Nes!" Bioti pulled away from his strong grip, her hands up and clenched, as if ready to fight. "If you had seen it—what Lord Kiralyn did to my husband—you would have been thinking, too. Aye, you would be doing a lot of thinking."

"Bioti, that was years ago." If she was reasonable, Nes might try to prove that, for once, he stood with Lord Kiralyn. Bioti's husband had usurped the lord's authority. Lord Kiralyn had every right to send him to the fields, just like he had sent dozens of other men. But no one expected Phillip to contract scurvy. The lord could not be blamed for that.

"You think I do not feel the pain every day? Phillip is dead because of Lord Kiralyn. He deserves to lose his daughter. To feel the pain of her absence every morn the sun rises."

Nes shook his head slowly. "He has already lost his wife." He knew too well how that felt.

"Aye." Bioti nodded her head, an evil smile creeping onto her face. "Even the hand of Providence is against him."

"Then let Providence take his child."

"Nay!" Bioti looked back at Ellia, who was watching the argument with wide eyes. She turned again to Nes, lowering her voice. "Have you never wanted a new life? A life where you didn't have to work so hard to gain too little? Look around you, Nes." She gestured with both arms.

Nes sighed and let his eyes travel around the child's room. Dark carpet covered the floor, scattered with fancy toys. A cradle stood in the corner, lined with a shiny material. There was more in this one place than in Nes's entire cottage, which he was forced to share with others, since he had no family.

"You can live better than you live today." Bioti's soft words drew his attention. "I have access to a whole chest of money."

"What is that to me?" Nes kept his voice indifferent as his eyes rested on the blonde head of a child who, as the daughter of a lord, would never experience toil or pain.

"It can all be yours. Dig yourself a grave too. Let people think you have died."

"And who would be there to report my death?" Nes scoffed.

Bioti shrugged. "I'm sure you can find a way to make it happen." Her gray eyes penetrated into Nes's, challenging him. "Journey to another village. Start a new life as a rich man. I promise: no one shall discover the truth." Bioti reached down and picked up the pouch. "This alone holds more coins than you ever see in a season, and you can have it all today."

"How do I know you will give me the rest?"

Bioti smiled. "Because you will walk away with it."

Nonsense. Nes brought his hands up to massage his aching neck as he watched Bioti reach under Ellia's lacy bed. She pulled out a trunk and thumped it with her fist.

"I cannot lift it, but you can." She tilted it enough for coins to tumble around on the inside.

Nes knelt beside the chest, secured with a lock. A passage out? Surely wishes didn't come true. Not for peasants. "'Tis your money?"

Bioti rolled her eyes. "What servant has this kind of money? Lord Kiralyn will not miss it nor will he miss you."

Nes's jaw tightened at her comment. If she was trying to remind him that he had no one to care for him in his old age, she wasn't missing her mark.

"The fine and mighty lord has enough to lend. Especially if it will guarantee the safety of his precious daughter." She straightened and picked up Ellia. "Take the chest. And if that is not enough, I shall see to it that you live comfortably for the rest of your pitiful life." Her jaw ticked tighter as she spoke.

Nes looked from the chest to Bioti. "You think I shall trust you?"

"Aye." Bioti's eyes flashed. "This is far better than anything Lord Kiralyn would do for you. When he returns, your chance will be gone."

"And the lass. She'll live?"

"If you take the money and flee, aye."

Nes held Bioti's gaze. "I will hold you to that."

Bioti smirked. She backed away from Nes and placed her hand on the door behind him. "Three graves. Cover them, then flee."

Chapter One

Ten Years Later

Kiralyn Castle

Raoul, lord of Kiralyn, turned to take one more look at the king's castle. King Jarin hadn't changed for the better since he had last seen him, when Belle had come to live at Kiralyn Castle. But Raoul couldn't argue Belle's decision to follow God and stay with her father, even though it left an aching hole in his heart.

He leaned forward and urged Malkyn to go faster, letting the wind lace itself through his hair. Focusing on riding stole his concentration from the heartache at hand, yet he couldn't stop his prayers from coming. "Father, I thought Thou hadst sent her to us…to fill the void we so desperately needed to be filled." His throat tightened. He couldn't begrudge the king his daughter, when, after all of these years, he still yearned to hold Ellia in his arms. "Father, let there be no bitterness in us."

Malkyn went through the gates of Kiralyn Castle before Raoul was ready. He led the horse to where the stable lad waited then swung to the ground.

"Did you have a fair trip, m'lord?"

It was a simple question, but it drove a stake deeper into Lord Kiralyn's heart. "Fair enough. Thank you." He ran up the steps to his castle, not stopping to admire the grandeur before him. It was a part of his life, but it had never been enough to have wealth. He had to have someone with whom he and Elayne could share it.

"Where is Lady Kiralyn?" Raoul asked as he entered.

The butler bowed. "In the parlor, m'lord."

Raoul slowed as he neared the parlor. Elayne had taken Belle completely under her wing, as if she was the daughter that Elayne could never have.

He stopped at the doorway and leaned his head against the frame. "Father, give me the right words." He waited for a few moments, steadying himself with several deep breaths.

"Raoul, is that you?"

Raoul suppressed a groan as he straightened and entered the sitting room. Elayne was seated near the window, embroidery in hand. Strong, yet elegant. He stepped closer as Elayne lifted her eyes to meet his.

"Have you been crying, my dear?" He quickened his pace.

"Percy came after you left."

"Ah." Raoul knelt before his wife, not knowing whether to feel relieved or distressed that the news had already been revealed. "Is it safe to assume he shared with you the same news that Belle told me?"

"Aye." Elayne nodded and took a shuddering breath. "'Tis right, isn't it?"

"I wish I could deny it, but she had such peace." He said the words as much for his benefit as for hers. "She sends you her love."

Silence stretched between them.

"I suppose we must move on."

"Aye." Raoul looked up at his wife. She fought to maintain a smile.

"Life certainly shan't be the same," Elayne said, rising and moving around the room, touching various items that didn't need to be straightened.

"We shall learn to live this way." His voice sounded flat, even to himself. But he couldn't grieve Elayne by baring his heart. The parlor seemed emptier, now that he knew Belle wouldn't be returning. He stood up. "I shall be in my study if you need me."

Remembrance flashed across Elayne's face. "Jolin is in the study. He said it was urgent business and that he would not leave until you returned."

"Send for Galien." Whatever the business, Raoul knew he'd need both men at his service. His stride quickened as he went through the halls. His study door was open. "What is it?" he asked, before fully entering the room.

Jolin closed the door and stood beside it, studying his hands as they rolled and unrolled the brim of his hat.

"Well?" Raoul went to his desk and sat down, laying his forearms on the surface in front of him. "I am ready for business, Jolin. Or shall we wait for Galien?"

Jolin walked to the chair opposite the desk, but didn't sit down. "I met one of your old servants, m'lord."

Raoul groaned and leaned back. How was this urgent? "The complaints of unjust dues. Really, Jolin, you ought to know how to handle those by now."

"Nay, m'lord." Jolin met Raoul's gaze, his blue eyes serious. "'Twas Nes."

Raoul's neck stiffened as the door opened, admitting Galien. "Should I remember him for any particular reason? He was my groundsman—"

"Who allegedly died in the plague." Jolin's blunt tone added force to his words.

Raoul lowered his voice, even though Galien had already closed the door. "You say he's alive?"

"Aye. He is asking for money."

"Why should the lord hand money to a servant?" Galien asked, settling into the chair beside Jolin, seeming to piece the conversation together. "You ought to make *him* pay, leaving under a guise."

"He says he's not the only servant who left behind an empty grave," Jolin said. "He'll give information…for a price."

"Get to the point, Jolin." Raoul couldn't explain the growing tension that threaded itself through his muscles. As far as he cared, Nes and the memories of the plague could be removed from his life.

"Bioti didn't die either." Jolin's fingers kneaded his hat again. "Nes says she took Ellia with her."

Chapter Two

Abtshire

Water sloshed over the sides of the pail, drenching Lia as she stumbled into the stables.

"Tardy again?" Dumphey's tones were light, but Lia glared at him.

"If it weren't for Geva and Helga, you know I would have been here earlier."

"Ah, 'twas your sisters then?"

"They are not *my* sisters," Lia hissed. She had told him dozens of times already. He couldn't see the tension that knotted in her stomach whenever she was linked to the spoiled daughters of Bioti.

Dumphey reached for the pail. "You spilt half of the water."

"I shall take another trip then." Lia frowned as she relinquished the pail.

"There isn't time for such. We shall have to let Noel go for it if needed."

Dumphey's long strides widened the space between them as he walked to the far end of the stables. Lia raised her voice as she hobbled after him, schooling her face to hide her wince. "Noel should despise me by now, always making more work for him. I shall get the second bucketful."

"And let Sheriff Feroci tend to the taxes with his equipment wet?" He lowered his voice and muttered, "These should have been done yesterday." He looked at her with a half smile. "You dust the saddle, and I shall wash the reins since I've dusted them already."

Heat burned in Lia's cheeks as she took a dry cloth and rubbed it over the leather. It was her task to dust both the saddle and the reins in the evenings after the sheriff returned…except she had to leave early last night at Bioti's demands and was late today. Again. If the sheriff knew how little she actually did the tasks assigned to her, he might recall his deal with Bioti and thrust them from their home. She shivered and added speed to her dusting.

"Slowly, Lia." Dumphey's tone was calm and gentle, as if she were a mere child. "You are to be thorough, not speedy."

Dumphey didn't have to add that Sheriff Feroci's man, Barat, would take a thorough look-over before accepting the tack for his master. Lia didn't know if it was the sheriff who was particular, or Barat. She clenched the rag tighter as she smoothed it across the leather. “You shall finish before me and be waiting.”

“Then I shall help you.”

The rag balled in her hands. She shook it out before applying it to the saddle again, this time with added force. Her breath pushed out between her clenched teeth. “You and Noel could get in trouble if you were ever found out.” Besides, she didn’t need them to go above and beyond, trying to help her.

Dumphey snorted. “We shall be careful.” His voice lowered. “We were raised to be careful around the likes of the sheriff.”

“If he ever finds out—”

“He shan’t.” Dumphey rinsed his rag in the bucket of water. “Stable work is not for a lass.”

Lia scowled at Dumphey, even though his head was bent and he couldn’t see her. He wasn’t that much older than her. She didn’t need his opinions. “I have no choice.”

Dumphey shook his head. “Bioti could have let two of you work instead of just one. That would provide funds enough for her to keep her lovely cottage.”

“Oh, but the sisters are too refined for such a task as this.” Bitterness laced her words, but she couldn’t hold it back. She folded the rag so that it would fit in the creases of the fancy-work carved into the saddle. “I wish I could see an end to this, but I know there isn’t one. Bioti will never seek more work if she knows she can appease the sheriff with me here."

Dumphey cleared his throat in a low warning. Lia bit her tongue and focused on the saddle as footsteps came through the stables.

"I don't believe I heard talking…?" The icy statement skittered through the stables like sleet on cobblestones.

Lia glanced up at Dumphey. His eyebrows lowered as he slid the reins through the rag in his hand.

"I thought not." Barat stood over Lia. Her hands shook as she cleaned another crevice. "I definitely didn't foresee you cleaning the tack this morn. Dumphey? The sheriff likes his tack clean." He paused and slid a finger over the leather. "Not wet."

"It will be done and dry before the sheriff needs it," Dumphey said, his voice strained as his hands worked faster. Lia matched his pace.

"I thought you left these tasks for…the lass?"

Dumphey's eyes flashed as he glanced at Lia before looking up at Barat. "You will find my tasks completed. I saw no harm in ensuring the tack was done correctly and in time." When he looked back at Lia, his hazel eyes begged forgiveness for shifting blame to her. She looked away.

Barat cleared his throat and walked back toward the door. He paused and spun on his heel.

"Oh, Dumphey, did I mention that the sheriff is wishing to leave early today?"

Dumphey's eyebrows lowered even further than earlier, if that was possible. "How early?"

"Within the hour."

The only response Dumphey gave was quickening his pace.

"I shall tell him he shan't be disappointed." Barat chuckled low and walked away, his footsteps echoing on the wooden planks.

As soon as the door shut behind Barat, Lia whispered, "Shall I get Noel?"

"Nay." Dumphey threw his rag into the pail as he stood up. "I shall be quicker. See if you can finish the seat before we return."

He left, and Lia swallowed back tears as her hands moved faster. He would never realize how much pain it caused to continually bring up her lameness. She wiped her eyes on her sleeve. Salty tears mustn't land on the saddle and leave their mark. She couldn't afford anything to slow her down further. Her slowness had already put Dumphey and Noel in potential trouble. She dusted off the last piece of leather before dunking her rag in the water. Her hands would have to compensate for the hours that Bioti stole from her. And she would work harder every morn so Bioti would release her sooner. She would prove to Dumphey that she could work hard, even with her limp.

Chapter Three

Kiralyn Castle

Raoul's heart hammered in his chest. "She can't be alive. All of the servants assured me she was dead. Nes himself buried…" Raoul stopped and massaged his forehead. The servants had reported that Nes had buried Ellia before he himself died, and Raoul never questioned it. It hadn't seemed important then. He had lost both Ellia and his wife Nydia.

Jolin moved behind the desk and placed his hand on Raoul's shoulder, not saying a word. Raoul closed his eyes for a moment. When he opened them, Jolin asked, "Shall I bring Nes here?"

Galien shook his head. "We needn't do anything rashly. 'Tis possible Nes fibbed, to gain more money."

Raoul heard a slight hesitation in his voice. He shifted in his chair then sat up, pulling his shoulder away from Jolin's gentle grasp. "Do you think that?"

Jolin shrugged.

"Why did you not demand answers then?"

"He gave the message, then left."

Raoul stood up and stepped away from Jolin, looking from one man to the other. "I want you to go back to Nes and do not return unless you bring him."

"What if he refuses to come?" Galien asked.

"Then give him the money."

Galien leaned forward. "You will toss money at a former servant—one who left his duties no less—just like that?"

Raoul crossed his arms. "If it were your daughter, would you not do the same?"

Galien stiffened and a mask slid over the pain in his brown eyes.

Raoul took in a quick breath. There was no excuse for his carelessness. "I beg forgiveness, Galien." He couldn't meet the man's eyes. No one had fibbed about the death of Galien's daughter during the plague. She had died the day before the men had returned.

Jolin cleared his throat and began slowly, "We could bring payment, show him the coins—"

Raoul looked at Jolin, wishing the discussion over.

"And if he is fibbing, you reward him?" Galien's voice was clipped and cold.

"Nay." Jolin's jaw was tight. His blue eyes bore into Raoul, as if reminding him of the many years he had wisely dealt with Raoul's business. "I wouldn't pay without proof, m'lord."

Raoul shrugged his shoulders as a pounding ache made its way into his head. "I will leave that to your discernment. Just go." He turned his back to them, knowing that they wouldn't press the issue further. He had to think this through while they were away. Find a better way to retrieve answers if Nes decided to be tight-lipped.

When the door shut behind the men, Raoul thrust his fingers through his hair and let out a lungful of air. He should tell Elayne…nay. Smoothing his hair back into place, he sped out the door. His footsteps pounded down the empty hallway as he caught up to Jolin and Galien.

"I'm going with you."

Jolin shook his head. "Nay, m'lord."

"Don't tell me nay." Raoul followed Jolin out to the courtyard. He checked his words as they passed by a few servants. "Jolin." He kept his voice low so that it couldn't be overheard. "I am going."

Jolin tilted his head toward the stables as he looked at Galien. "Ready two horses."

Raoul gripped Jolin's shoulder as Galien left. "Sometimes you enrage me."

Jolin nodded. "And sometimes you are too hasty."

"We can plan our next step as we ride together."

No response.

Raoul shook Jolin. "Give me three good reasons why I should remain here."

Jolin looked down at his boots. His shoulders rose then fell under Raoul's grip before he looked up. "M'lord, you are angry. I fear you shall do something you will regret."

"That is one reason."

"Aye." Jolin brought his gaze up to meet Raoul's. "That one is enough."

Raoul shoved Jolin and stomped past him as Galien came out with two horses. He grabbed the bridle of one. *No father on earth would let his daughter out of sight longer than necessary. Especially if she were in the hands of Bioti. But you wouldn't understand that.*

Jolin walked past Raoul, grabbed the pommel, and hoisted himself onto the horse's back. He leaned down and kept his voice low. "When we know more, then we can discuss the next step."

Raoul's fingers tightened on the reins of Jolin's horse. He looked from one man to the other.

"You can trust us, m'lord," Galien said, his face serious.

"Stay," Jolin said. "Talk with Lady Kiralyn. Pray together."

Raoul's ears throbbed with each word the men said. He blinked to focus. *One would think I had no control over my servants…* Yet he couldn't believe that, even in his anger. Jolin was more than a servant. He had proven that in the past, when Raoul's anger had kept him from seeing reason before.

"M'lord." Galien's voice was soft. "It is not likely that Nes knows where she is—or mayhap he is not being truthful. It will take more than one visit to find…" he let his voice fade as he glanced around the courtyard, "her."

Raoul's fingers unclamped the reins only to clench into fists. He spun on his heel and stormed back to the castle. He would let the men leave, and he would follow behind. Then they couldn't keep him from interrogating Nes himself.

He passed through the halls in mere seconds, his footsteps thundering against the stone floor. Stopping in front of the nursery door, he let out a slow, shaky breath as his fists loosened. He reached for the handle. It turned easily, and the door creaked open. Light from the hall window peeked into the dark bedchamber. Raoul pushed the door open until a bright path shone from the hall to the chamber's windows. He crossed the room and pulled open the curtains, letting in more rays of light. He stood for a moment, staring out the window. It had been years since he had seen this view from the castle. Ten years, to be exact. But it was easier to look down at the land he daily walked on than to turn to face Ellia's empty room and wonder what had become of her.

"Raoul?" Elayne's voice was soft. Her arms wrapped around him. "You have never been in here since our marriage." Her voice dropped even lower. "Is it Belle's absence?" A tinge of sadness laced her voice as she laid her head on his shoulder.

Raoul placed his hands on top of Elayne's, wishing her calmness could ease the wound that had reopened after all these years.

"Where are they going?" Elayne moved from Raoul's grasp.

Raoul cleared his throat as he followed Elayne's gaze to Galien and Jolin riding away. He would follow after talking with Elayne. She had been his steady supporter ever since he had told her of his first wife's and Ellia's deaths. How would she react to the news of Ellia being alive? *If she is alive,* Raoul reminded himself.

Elayne turned and raised her eyebrows. "Is something the matter?"

Raoul's throat went dry. He tried clearing it again, wishing the action would also calm his racing heart. "El—" his lips wouldn't form the name he hadn't spoken in years. He turned away from Elayne and watched the dust particles floating in the light. He strode across the room and looked into Ellia's crib. His arm brushed the lace as he reached in to clasp the slipper that rested among the blankets. It lay in his palm, dainty and light, like Ellia had been as a child. Where was she today at…thirteen? He turned the blanket over until he found the other slipper. It was twisted to conform to the only foot that would fit into it—Ellia's.

He turned to face Elayne. "They say she's alive."

Elayne's eyes widened. "Who says?"

"Jolin…one of my old servants, Nes." He paused to straighten his thoughts. "We thought Nes was dead. He's not. He told Jolin that the nursemaid took…Ellia."

Elayne stepped to his side and slipped her hand on his arm. "Did they unearth the graves?"

Raoul jerked to study his gentle, proper wife. "Dig up…" He couldn't finish.

"Aye." Now, she flushed, as she apparently realized the meaning of her suggestion. "Mayhap you could begin with Nes's and Bioti's...to ensure they are not there." Her words rushed as she continued, "You may wait until Jolin and Galien have returned then—"

"Nay." Raoul took a deep breath as he looked down at the slippers. "We shall do it."

Chapter Four

Abtshire

Lia pushed the door open and slipped through it, into the outdoor air. She took a deep breath, trying not to smell anything. The stables smelled better than this part of the village, where scraps and trash filled every spare corner. Holding a hand to her nose, she walked away from Bioti's wattle and daub cottage.

"Lia! Where are you?"

Lia released her breath. She knew better than try to outrun Bioti. The older woman could chase her down unless she was out of sight. She choked as her lungs involuntarily took in enough air to last her until she reached inside.

"What do you think you're doing?"

"I'm on my way to the stables," Lia said, keeping her eyes focused on the ground beneath her long skirts as she walked back inside the dim cottage. Her fingers curled into a loose ball as she clenched her teeth. She relaxed the next moment. She shouldn't be showing Bioti her feelings.

Bioti let out a frustrated groan. "'Tis barely into the morn. You have sufficient time to knead the bread before heading out."

"I was late yestermorn." Lia kept her voice low as she hobbled to the table, where she had left the dough to rise. Of course she shouldn't have expected that Bioti would make Geva finish the task. The lass was still in bed.

"Always shirking." Bioti placed her fists on her plump waist. "Do not make me hire you out for a servant. And that will happen if I do not find someone to marry you by sixteen."

Lia gritted her teeth and pounded the dough. She wouldn't put it past Bioti to hire her out before she was sixteen. She forced herself to be gentle. The bread wouldn't rise if she was harsh with it, which would then mean Bioti would make her skip dinner.

"I wonder if the sheriff's wife might find use for ye," Bioti said, settling onto a chair. Lia glanced sideways at her. One day, that chair would decide to give out under her weight. Which meant that Lia would be blamed, even though she had nothing to do with it being rickety. Bioti leaned back, making the chair moan. "Mayhap I could speak with her. Wish me luck that she doesn't ask to examine you before accepting your service." The last words were spoken in a harsh grumble.

Heat rolled into Lia's cheeks. She tried to feign a smile, wishing it would erase this telltale sign of her discomfort. "I do not believe the sheriff could do with one less stable hand, and I cannot do them both."

Bioti stood, knocking the chair over. Lia took a step back, but Bioti was faster, slapping her cheek.

"Do not backtalk me, child!"

Lia blinked back sudden tears as her stomach cinched. *Show nothing. It doesn't hurt me. It doesn't.* She bit her tongue as she pinched the dough into loaves and flung them onto the stone. She forced her words to come out evenly as she said, "These are ready for baking when they have risen." She smeared the dough from her hands to her apron. "I shall be late." She didn't wait for Bioti to reply. Hopping on her good leg, she reached the door.

"Helpless child. No one shall want you!"

She slammed the door and spun around. Ignoring the pain that shot up through her leg, she stumbled through the streets. This time, she didn't even notice the smells. She swallowed, trying to release the lump in her throat, but it only made it worse.

One day, I shall show Bioti. 'Tis her own daughters who are helpless. If it weren't for me…

Lia left the thought unfinished as she reached the stables. She could hear the spade scraping ground and groaned. Someone had begun mucking the stalls—the task she was supposed to do.

She swung open the door. "Dumphey, I—"

"No need for excuses, Lia." Dumphey tossed a spadeful of manure into the barrow then held out the spade to her. He gave her a small grin. "Just giving you a head start before Philaon arrives."

Lia wrapped her fingers around the handle and dipped her head. That hateful blush was returning, she could feel it. She didn't need people to give her head starts. She could do it on her own. "I'm thankful it's Philaon and not Barat who oversees us."

"Which could change any day."

Memories of Barat's unexpected visit the day before sent a shiver through Lia as she entered a stall. She filled her spade—much less than what Dumphey had done—then added it to the barrow.

"Call me when it needs emptying," Dumphey said over his shoulder as he left Lia alone.

It had probably taken Dumphey a few minutes to empty the first stall, while it took Lia half an hour to scrape clean the second stall he had begun. For every half-minute she saved by moving the spade quickly, she lost in her stumbled trip to the barrow.

"Good morn." The young, cheery voice belonged to Noel.

Lia straightened. She smiled as Noel's hair fell over

his eyes. He brushed the brownish-blond strands back impatiently then clasped his spade with both hands.

"My tasks are complete, may I help you, m'lady?" He gave a low bow, flourishing his hand.

A giggle escaped Lia, though she could feel her cheeks flaming. Why were Dumphey and Noel trying so hard? Their extra efforts as much as said she was more of a hindrance than a help. She thrust the spade into the mixture of hay and dung. If mucking the stalls could be done in one position, she wouldn't be so slow. Perhaps she could talk with Dumphey about reassigning her tasks. She shook her head. She was going to prove her worth, not ask for more help.

She tried to match Noel's pace, which only increased the heat in her face and the pain in her leg. The younger lad was almost twice as fast as she.

When Noel left to find Dumphey to empty the barrow, Lia leaned against the spade, glaring at the stall in front of her. Why did everything in life have to be so difficult?

"Lia!"

Lia winced at the high-pitched squeal of Geva's voice and turned. "I am busy."

"I think not." Geva lifted her nose into the air. "I saw you resting."

"Waiting for Dumphey to come empty the barrow."

"Empty it yourself, you idle lass." Geva stamped her foot to add emphasis to her words.

Lia glared at the girl, several years younger than her. "I am not idle—"

"Mother says you are and I believe Mother—not you."

Of course she did. She was just like Bioti. Lia turned to the next stall, even though she could do nothing more than fill her spade while waiting for the lads. "What are you doing here?"

"Mother insists you come see her."

Lia threw up one of her hands. "I am to work here to pay off her debts so she can stay in her lovely cottage." She let sarcasm drip off her tongue before hardening her voice. "I cannot leave or we will be removed from our home."

Geva sniffed in disdain. "Mayhap Mother has gotten you another job."

"So soon?" The spade dropped from her grasp.

Geva skipped forward and grabbed Lia's hand. "Come now, lest I drag you through this muck. I doubt Lady Yzebel would take kindly to a mucked-up servant girl." She cackled as if she had made a jest.

Lady Yzebel? Servant girl? What happened to Bioti waiting until she was near sixteen? Lia glanced behind her as she stumbled to keep up with Geva. Dumphey and Noel were not in sight. Would they think that she had fled her task? They were the only friends she had—she couldn't afford to lose them over a whim of Bioti's.

Chapter Five

Kiralyn Castle

"We found him," Jolin said as he entered the study. He shut the door behind Galien.

"You found him," Raoul repeated, his tone flat and dull. "That *was* your goal." He bolted from his chair, bringing him eye-to-eye with the men. "What did he *say*?"

"He was…reluctant," Galien said, taking a step back and shifting his gaze from Raoul's.

Raoul glared at Jolin. "I thought you said he would speak for money?" Nes *had* to speak for money.

"M'lord, just listen."

Raoul clenched his jaw as he crossed his arms and touched his back to the bookcase behind him. The external feign of relaxation did nothing to calm his nerves. Ellia wasn't in the grave, like he had been led to believe these ten years. Where was she?

"I gave him the money." Galien hesitated and fidgeted with his shirt, still not bringing his eyes to meet Raoul's gaze. "He said to look in Matheny."

Raoul threw his hands up. "Look in Matheny? Does he know how vast the city is? How much did you pay him? We need direct answers, Galien. Not leads. And I thought you were to bring him to me?"

"He refused to come." Galien shifted. "He didn't give the information until after I handed him the sack."

Raoul stood up. "Order three horses saddled. We're going together."

"M'lord." Jolin gestured to the window. "Nighttime is falling."

"Aye," Raoul said. Insufferable man. Next, he would remind Raoul that the two had already made the rounds to and from Fordyce today, that they were tired and needed a full night's rest. Raoul pushed the consideration aside. "The carriage, then. You may sleep as we ride."

Galien stood and left, leaving the door to slam behind him.

Jolin walked to the bookcase and leaned his arm against it, staring at Raoul until he looked at him. One glance at his serious blue eyes, and Raoul looked away, his gaze falling on the silk slipper he had placed on his desk. He had meant to move it before the men returned.

"What is the likelihood of childhood deformities healing themselves?" Raoul's thoughts came out in a low murmur. He cleared his throat and shifted positions, away from Jolin. It was too late to retrieve the question.

"I know not, m'lord."

Another pause. Raoul tried to bring his thoughts into a prayer, just like he had all day. Instead of prayers, he only had questions. Questions without answers.

"Raoul…"

If it were any of his other servants, Raoul could reprimand him for impertinence. But not Jolin. He had been like a brother to Raoul all these years, when his own brother, the king, refused to see him. When Jolin didn't continue, Raoul grunted. "Say it."

"I believe you should reconsider tonight's journey."

Raoul's back stiffened.

"Have you even discussed this with Lady—"

"I see that as none of your concern."

"Have you remembered tomorrow's—"

"They can wait."

"What of highwaymen?"

Here, Raoul couldn't find an answer. He swallowed and sucked in a lungful of air. It wasn't enough oxygen. He inhaled again.

"Postpone the trip less than twelve hours, m'lord."

Raoul clenched his teeth and balled his fingers into fists.

"With all consideration, it has already been so long. A few more hours—"

Raoul's fist rammed the shelf, the bang making Jolin jump. "It was ten years without our knowledge of her. She wasn't buried, Jolin. Her grave is empty." There, the words were out. He turned away from Jolin. He didn't want to see his reaction. "What has Nes done besides telling us she's alive? Or Bioti? What has she done to Ellia?" He clenched his fist tighter to mask that his limbs were shaking. What if Nes was holding something back?

"M'lord, we must trust God in this. He has kept her these ten years. Cannot He keep her another night?" Jolin's voice was low and solid.

Raoul turned to look beyond Jolin. The slipper came into focus again. He licked his lips then choked out, "No later than dawn."

Chapter Six

Abtshire

Bioti walked in front of Lia, as if purposefully blocking her stilted gait from Lady Yzebel's view as they approached. Lia's feet sank into the rich depth of the plush carpet. She forced herself to keep from wiggling her toes and burying her feet further into the soothing embrace as she waited for the sheriff's wife.

"Is this the daughter of whom you spoke?"

The gentle words slipped like ice through Lia's veins. She bit her tongue before she contradicted the lady. Bioti found no qualms in claiming Lia as her own in public, though she treated her as nothing when in private.

"She is a hard worker, a gentle lass. I know that you shall find her suited to all of your needs." How did Bioti manage to sound like an endearing, partial mother in front of Lady Yzebel? Lia kept her eyes glued on the deep red tones of the carpet to keep from glaring at Bioti. "Come here, Lia." Bioti stepped aside and pushed Lia forward to let Lady Yzebel look her over.

Lia buried her hands in the folds of Geva's gown, the soft linen not calming her at all. She made sure her steps were slow and even, making her appear the careful lass Bioti claimed her to be. Had she not spent the last hour transitioning from filthy rags to this pale green gown, she would have doubted that she was the same lass mucking the stalls this morn. She lifted her eyes, taking in every embroidered flower that decorated the deep gray silk of Lady Yzebel's gown. The beauty of elegance stopped as she looked at the lady's face.

Lady Yzebel's brows furrowed, enough to show a touch of disapproval, yet not enough to cast away her façade of grace. "Haven't you sensible attire?"

Lia blushed and crossed her hands behind her. "Yes, m'lady."

"Good. I am in need of a kitchen maid. 'Twouldn't do to have you strutting in the kitchen with fancier attire than the other maids."

Bioti's eyes flashed. "I thought she was to be your personal maid?" She kept her voice cool, but Lia could see that beneath the polite retort, she was holding back her rage.

"Madame, you asked for an opening, and this is where I have one." Lady Yzebel pulled out her embroidery. "You may return to the kitchen door. Within the hour, or the opening will be given to another maid."

"Yes, m'lady." Lia held her breath as she lowered into a steady curtsy. Beneath the length of the dress, she had to plant her feet solidly on the floor and bend her knees to make the appearance of an elegant curtsy. Nothing like what she was told real ladies were trained to do. But then, she was not a real lady, nor would she ever be one.

Bioti huffed as she grabbed hold of Lia's hand. "We shall get her into suitable clothes at once and she shall return to assist your staff. At the price we agree upon."

Lady Yzebele didn't return so much as a glance in their direction.

Bioti walked slowly until they left the room. Then, she dragged Lia along.

"You already agreed upon a price for—for me?"

Bioti turned enough for Lia to see her lips turned into a harsh frown. "Don't question my methods, Lia."

"You do realize that this could likely break your deal with the sheriff." She limped as she spoke. If only Bioti would keep her pace considerate.

"Nay. You shall do both."

"Both?" Lia stopped and pulled her hand away from Bioti. "Have you gone mad? If I die I am of no use to anyone!"

"Do not talk to me in that manner! You shall do as I say. And if you do not do *well* at what I say, you shall regret it."

"You have two daughters who are fully able to—"

A sharp sting interrupted Lia. She clenched her fists to keep from bringing them up to sooth her smarting face. One day, she would make Bioti regret the many times she slapped her.

"They are my *daughters.* You are not. It is your fault I have need of extra money. Not theirs. Now hurry or we shall lose this opportunity." Bioti charged toward her cottage.

Lia pressed her tongue on the roof of her mouth to force back tears as she followed, not even trying to keep up with Bioti's angry stride. When Bioti was several paces away, Lia stopped and massaged her foot. Why did Mama have to die, leaving Papa lonely enough to marry someone like Bioti? And then, why had Papa died before she could even remember his loving face? She was sure that he had been loving, not like Bioti's second husband who was kind only when something would benefit his selfish heart. Still, nothing good had come from his death. In the days when Bioti's husband was alive, Lia remembered living almost as fine as the sheriff himself. That had faded quickly once he died, leaving Bioti even more bitter, now that she had three lasses relying on her alone.

Lia entered the house without a word and changed into her own cotton garments, well-suited for kitchen work. Or any work, for that case. Not much could stain them more than they had been stained already. Any profit that Lia had gleaned in working for Bioti went for things for Geva and Helga, unless Lia's garb was too threadbare to be of use. *I do not see how it's my fault Bioti needs more money. She never uses the extra money for me anyway.*

"Hurry, child. You will be back there within the half hour or no dinner for you."

Lia left the house without a word, her brain boiling. *If it weren't for me, there would* be *no dinner.* She turned onto the next street, her body plunging into someone. She reached for the air as she lost her balance and fell to the ground, her crippled foot pinned underneath her. She let out a cry.

"Forgive me, lass. I wasn't looking where I was going."

Strong arms grasped her wrists before she could respond. Pushing them away would only mean falling back, helpless to the ground, so Lia accepted. She kept her eyes averted, hiding the tears that she knew were visible, as she was helped back to her feet.

"Can you walk?"

Lia swallowed and blinked to push the tears back. She glanced at the man before her, enough to acknowledge him, but not enough to reveal the pain she was in. He wasn't from around these areas. Given his posture and manner, she doubted he was her class either.

"Aye." She pulled her hands from his grasp and took a few steps away, her ankle twisting. She winced as she felt her body show evidence of her limp.

"Did you hurt your foot?"

If that was all he thought, she was safe. "Mayhap a little. I beg pardon…sir." Lia wished she knew the proper way to address this man. "I mayn't be late. The ankle will heal." She held her breath as she stepped forward at a steady pace. Every step hurt worse than usual.

Where were her manners? She turned around after a few steps. "I thank you…sir." She didn't wait for his response. A flash of pity had gone through his face—pity that she had seen often in others' eyes and hated. At least he thought her pain was temporary.

Lia shook the thoughts from her mind. She had work before her, and after she was released from the kitchen, she had to return to the stables and explain some things to Dumphey.

Chapter Seven

Abtshire

Raoul looked after the lass, still limping from her recent fall. Guilt filled him.

"Should I offer her assistance?" He had to focus on where he was, who was around him, to avoid another collision.

"The villagers are proud and do not need help from their superiors." Jolin laid a hand on Raoul's arm. "If we wish to arrive at Matheny before nightfall, we mustn't tarry."

Raoul sighed as he looked around at the cottages, the guilt still not easing from his chest. "One would think a lord would see better to the needs of his vassals. How many of these villages are in Lord Trey's domain?"

"I know not. They seem satisfied enough, aye?"

Raoul glanced back at the lass, now a distance away. Her limp was still visible. It would take days for it to heal, considering the way she favored it while walking. He had read pain in her face—of course, that may have been due to him causing her injury. But beneath that was fear. Worry. Turmoil. Not satisfaction.

"She's just one lass, Raoul." It was as if Jolin had read his mind. "Look at the others around here. You are not to judge another lord's land." His voice was gentle as he led the way back to the carriage.

"Aye." Raoul ran his fingers through his hair as he followed Jolin. He had enough of his own concerns without adding Lord Trey's domain to it. He followed Jolin to the carriage.

"I thought we had left Galien here." Jolin looked around with a frown before he jumped into the carriage and landed into a seat.

Raoul waited for the carriage to stop shaking before climbing in. He leaned back against the cushions and shut his eyes. Mayhap they should not have stopped in Abtshire. It would have spared them ten minutes—or longer, if Galien didn't hurry—as well as the young lass's pain because of his carelessness. He reached inside his pockets, letting his fingers rest against Ellia's silk slipper. They were still two cities away from where he would find her. Or, where he hoped he would find her.

The carriage shook again.

"Sorry for the delay, m'lord." Galien's voice filled the carriage as he shut the door.

Raoul opened one eye as the carriage jerked forward. Jolin was eyeing Galien. Raoul shook his head. He knew that look—the one that meant things were not going exactly how Jolin thought they should.

"What were you doing?" Now for Jolin's interrogation.

"Refilling the water." Galien looked out the window as they left the town. He sounded weary. "It was dirty."

"Did you see anything of interest?"

Galien never moved his focus from the scenery outside the window. "Nay. Just commoners."

"But a commoner is who we are looking for!" Raoul leaned forward and winced as his head pounded. He shut his eyes again and leaned into the sway of the carriage.

When Galien didn't reply, Raoul peeked at him. He was still staring at Abtshire. He shrugged as he looked back at Raoul. "'Tis a nice village."

Raoul groaned and closed his eyes. So Galien hadn't noticed anything that led him to Ellia. "Don't wake me 'til Matheny." He doubted he would get any sleep—he hadn't the night before—but trying would at least pass the time easier.

Chapter Eight

Abtshire

Lia placed another mushroom in her basket. The cook had said to fill it as full as possible without the mushrooms toppling to the ground or bruising. Given that the wicker basket was deep and wide, it would have a good weight by the time Lia brought it back.

She glanced up at the sunlight flickering through the trees. There was no Noel or Dumphey here to help speed up her labor so that she could take a slow, less-painful walk back—especially since her foot was throbbing from running into the man earlier.

She put both hands to work, breaking off a mushroom with each hand, but her clumsy fingers poked through the tender meat of the fungus. She tossed the damaged mushroom aside. No one needed to tell her that Sheriff Feroci expected nothing but the best served at his table.

She couldn't stop to think. She had to work, and carefully at that.

The heat of the day had lifted by the time she was walking out of the forest. Still, she had draped a light cloth over the mushrooms to keep the sun from kissing their cheeks. Her fingers clenched the basket until they ached, but she couldn't drop it.

"From stables to woods, I see."

Lia grasped the basket tighter, if possible.

"You cannot just leave like that."

"Dumphey…" Lia turned and looked up at the older lad. His patience must be wearing thin, even though he wore a grin. "I promise, 'twasn't me. I would have told you had I the chance."

"Will you be back or do Noel and I need to take up for you now?" Dumphey didn't sound accusing, but Lia stiffened as he pried the basket from her hands.

Lia kept her fingertips on the rim of the basket. "You needn't do this." She knew he wouldn't heed her words, but she felt the need to say them anyway.

Dumphey shrugged. "I'm empty-handed walking back to the village. What has Bioti done with you this time?" His earnest eyes met her gaze.

Lia looked away and focused on walking smoothly while keeping up with Dumphey's stride, though he had slowed down for her. "I shall return this evening. Leave chores for me. You have my word, I shall do it."

She glanced at Dumphey, long enough to see his mouth turn down in a frown.

"'Tis too much work for a lass your age."

"I shall have to make do." Or do without dinner, which might be the situation anyway if she didn't hurry.

"Hasn't Bioti any goodness in her heart for one of your condition?"

Lia stopped and grabbed Dumphey's arm, turning him to face her as the hateful blush heated her cheeks. "What of my condition? I make well enough most of the time." Her voice turned hard. "You needn't feel sorry for me, Dumphey." She snatched the basket from his hands, sending the cloth flying to the ground. She would run away from him if she could. Instead, she limped as quickly as her feet would let her, keeping herself from crying out in the pain.

"I shall leave the lights for you to polish." Dumphey's voice was well behind her. Good. He wasn't chasing her.

"I shall do it," Lia called, not bothering to turn back and make sure Dumphey got her message.

Her dark blonde hair was plastered to her forehead by the time she returned to the kitchen, and she panted for breath.

"Be the highwayman after you?" The cook took the basket from Lia and looked inside. "You are almost too late. There are potatoes waiting to be scrubbed and diced. Quickly."

Lia took the hint and hobbled to the table, where she grabbed a potato and began washing. Her fingers flew over the skins, making up for lost time. She would show Dumphey. She wasn't a worthless lass. She could do the tasks given her, regardless of what he thought.

Chapter Nine

Matheny

"I feel as if we have been led astray." Raoul heaved a sigh as he said the words. He had lost count of how many cottages he had been to in Matheny, which didn't include the ones that Jolin and Galien had visited.

"We haven't traversed the entire city yet," Jolin said, his tones light and cheerful. He led the way to the next row of cottages.

Raoul scowled at him. "Don't tell me what I haven't done. You said yourself that the way to glean information was to start with the servants and peasants. And have any of them heard of Bioti? Nay!"

"M'lord, 'tis a big city," Galien reasoned. "Surely not everyone knows of her."

Raoul stopped walking and held up his hands. "Nay, but 'tisn't likely that half of Matheny is ignorant of her!"

Galien shrugged. "What else do you propose to do?"

"I don't trust Nes. I am going to speak with him." It was what he should have done in the first place.

Galien's eyebrows shot up. "He won't speak without more coins."

"I don't care about the coins. Ellia is my daughter. I will do whatever it takes to find her."

"Are you not being rash?" Jolin asked. "What if one more day would find Bioti here?"

Bury the man. Raoul could count on him for his steady faithfulness, but that same steadiness would be his undoing one day. Jolin would not understand. He had never even had a wife to care for.

"What if one of us stayed behind?" Galien asked.

"Aye," Jolin agreed. "If you are willing to pay Nes for more information, hiring an extra horse for someone to stay here will be of no consequence. I can stay, m'lord."

"Nay, I'll stay."

Raoul and Jolin turned to look at Galien.

"But you were the one who spoke with Nes the other morn," Jolin said.

Galien gave a half-shrug. "Aye, and you see where that led us."

"Scared of him?" Jolin asked, the corner of his mouth twitching up.

"We haven't time to bicker." Raoul's tones were harsher than he intended, but it stopped the men. He started back toward the inn, taking longer strides than were proper. Each footstep jarred his throbbing head. He would have to try to rest on the few hours' ride to Fordyce.

"I'll call for the carriage," Galien said as they reached the inn.

"Very well." Raoul grimaced. Next time, he would bring Malkyn so he could come and go as he pleased instead of waiting a half hour.

They passed through the noisy dining hall and entered their dim room.

Jolin sighed. "M'lord, I fear you are annoyed."

"Annoyed?" Raoul choked on the word as he sank into a chair.

Jolin shrugged. At least, that is what it looked like from the slight illumination as Jolin lit the candles. The tallow tapers gave more smoke than they did light. "Infuriated, more like it?"

Raoul propped his feet on the straw mattress that rested on a wooden frame. It sagged as if giving a pathetic apology for keeping him awake the past two nights.

Jolin turned from the candles. "M'lord…" He walked to the small window and looked out. There wasn't much to see from that angle—mayhap a few cottage thatches—but he stared as if something caught his interest. Or because he didn't want to look Raoul in the eye.

"Say it." Raoul didn't have the patience to wait for Jolin to get to his point.

"I understand that I'm not a father, nor can I understand what you must be feeling; however…" Jolin massaged his chin, which had become scruffy in the past few days.

Raoul held his breath, bracing himself for words he knew he didn't want to hear, whatever they were.

Jolin looked squarely at Raoul. "Have you sought God in all of this?"

His breath released in a huff. If Jolin hadn't prefaced his speech so smoothly, Raoul would argue Jolin's inadequacy to make any comment. The man was too thorough. Raoul shut his eyes and leaned back, swallowing the dozens of hateful words with which he wanted to pound Jolin.

It wasn't Jolin he was angry with. Raoul rubbed his forehead. He couldn't make sense of anything right now, the way it was throbbing. He knew without opening his eyes that Jolin was patiently awaiting an answer. "I am seeking God," he said.

Jolin made no comment, but Raoul could feel him eyeing him with doubt. Let the man doubt, he would seek God on the way to Fordyce.

Chapter Ten

Abtshire

Lia took off her kitchen apron. She didn't want to soil it in the stables, even if all she had to do was polish lights. Dumphey had left her the same, simple task the past three days. She swallowed her annoyance and paused for a moment to look at the sunset. Last night, dark reds had entwined with orange, mellowing into the blue of the night sky. Tonight, it was a blank sheet of gray. With a sigh, she continued toward the stables. She didn't have time to waste looking at the paintings of nature around her.

A lone figure stood in front of the stable doors. Lia groaned. She had managed to talk civilly with Dumphey since his help with the mushrooms, but today she didn't want to converse with anyone.

"Lia!" The shrill whisper made Lia groan. Having Helga waiting for her was even worse than talking with Dumphey or Noel. "Mother insists on seeing you this instant."

"Helga, I have stable duties to fulfill." Lia tried to push past her.

"Aye, she knows that." Helga held out her arm and reached for Lia's hand. Lia pulled it away.

"Can it not wait until after my tasks are done?"

"Nay. She is in terrible straits this eve." She lowered her voice. "Or has been…ever since she had that visitor."

"Visitor?"

Helga shook her head and stood tall. "Never you mind. She is not apt for patience."

"Is she ever?" Lia muttered the words, but they were loud enough for Helga to hear.

"You could lose dinner for that."

"Only if she hears of it." Lia tried to glare at her step-sister, but the lass was taller than Lia, though she was four years younger.

"I'm not afraid of you. Catch me if you can!" With that, Helga spun around and dashed into the night.

Lia clenched her jaw until her teeth hurt. Heat pounded in her cheeks, and she reached up to rub them, even though there were no passersby to see. She refused to let others notice her discomfort. She hurried her walk and entered the cottage well after Helga had gone in and repeated the words that had passed between them.

"Child, one day you will learn respect." Bioti glared at Lia dangerously. "I don't have time for you tonight. I want you to return to the stables and harness a horse to a cart."

"Why?"

"Just do it!"

Lia crossed her arms and stood in front of Bioti. "I am not allowed to harness the horse." She watched as Bioti balled up some linens. "Is Sheriff Feroci casting us out?"

"No—yes!" Bioti stood, huffing from her efforts. "He said for us to use his horse and leave. Immediately."

Doubt crept through Lia. "Sheriff Feroci wouldn't let any commoner use his—"

"There is no need for me to answer your questions. Just do as I say. We have to be gone by tonight, and we could never make good time on foot. Especially with you." Lia bit back her response as Bioti continued, "You know the stables. Move…*quickly*." Bioti's gaze shot down to where Lia's skirts hid her foot.

Lia spun and darted out the door. She would show Bioti. She slammed the door on Bioti's harsh voice demanding her daughters to help. She retraced her steps to the stables, her heart pounding. She would be there tonight, as expected. But to steal? Her heart skipped a beat. *As if Sheriff Feroci gave permission.* That would never happen. If the sheriff caught her, or if Dumphey heard of it…

Just don't get caught. She eased the stable door open and looked behind her. *Run.* She could take a horse and flee the opposite direction of Bioti. It wasn't the first time the thought had crossed her mind. She had foolishly tried to run away as a younger child. She should have known better. The lesson Bioti gave her then sealed her fate: she would always be under Bioti's rule. She had no choice unless a man took pity on her and married her.

Lia ground her teeth. She wouldn't subject any man to that. She slipped inside the stable and let the door close behind her. What would happen when Bioti realized she wasn't returning with a cart? *She would report me as having stolen the horse for sure, and send the sheriff's men after me.* A shiver slipped up Lia's spine. She knew the penalty for horse thieving. *I could never run away.*

Everything was quiet except for the horses' greetings. Lia held her breath as she neared the stalls. Hauch wasn't her favorite, but he was fast and groomed for the cart.

"Come, Hauch." Lia led him from the stall, looking around as she did so. The cart was outside, used for common things. Lia could only hope the trappings were as easy to find. Her eyes flitted around the wall where the tack hung. She reached up and examined a few pieces before finding the harnesses. She removed them from their peg and draped them over her shoulder, wincing at the extra weight.

She placed a hand on Hauch's muzzle as she led him out of the stable. *Walk confidently, as if this is your task.*

The townspeople were used to her working at the stables by now. But still, her throat dried and her lungs refused to take in air. She backed Hauch next to the cart and lifted the harness from her shoulder. She placed it over Hauch's broad back and moved without a sound, hooking up the straps. Someone was likely to be disappointed to find their cart missing, but Lia couldn't answer to them.

She moved faster and the harness clanged against itself. She froze. The night around her was still silent. No one raised an alarm.

Before leading Hauch into the open, she stepped onto the street. She didn't recognize the few passersby. She could only hope that Dumphey or Noel wouldn't think to check in on her. She placed a shaking hand on the seat and pulled herself up. Her good foot slipped and she clamped her teeth to stop her cry. She tried again, this time making it up. She took the reins in her trembling hands. She couldn't make herself speak an encouragement to the horse. A simple slap would have to do.

Hauch stepped forward and the cart creaked. It was loaded, probably for the next day's market. Bioti would have to figure out what to do with that. Lia only had to get Hauch into Bioti's hands.

Once on the street, she lowered her head and let her hair fall over her face. There wasn't much light here, but she wasn't going to take chances.

"You're out late tonight."

The husky voice made Lia jump and tighten her hold on the reins. Without looking at the man, she kept her voice low and replied, "A task for the sheriff." It was just the town watch. He had seen her at the stables before.

"Couldn't wait 'til the morrow?"

Lia dared to look at him, feigning boldness she didn't feel. "Nay. You know the sheriff."

Hauch stepped into a light-footed trot, putting distance between them and the stables. In less than five minutes, Lia stopped at Bioti's cottage and looked over her shoulder. No one was watching her. She released the reins and stepped from the cart. Her foot caught and she fell to the ground. This time, her cry escaped.

The door flung open.

"Hush!" Helga's warning wasn't quiet itself. "Mother, she's back."

Bioti and Geva were out before the words left Helga's mouth.

"Get back up there." Bioti pulled Lia to her feet. "You're driving."

Chapter Eleven

Fordyce

Night was deepening when they neared Fordyce. The carriage slowed and Raoul sat up. "Finally!" He winced as pain sliced through his temples. The hours of jolting across the roads had done nothing to ease the tension.

"Where are we going now?" he asked.

Jolin straightened. "I gave the driver instructions to find Glenn Hollow. I figured the walk from there would do us both well."

"And how deep into Fordyce is this place?"

Jolin glanced out the window. "It should not be long."

Raoul followed Jolin's glance. The townspeople were hurrying around, as if trying to race against the fading daylight. The carriage passed by a group of children, racing to greet their father, who must have returned from a journey. Raoul swallowed and looked away, keeping himself from reaching into his pocket where his daughter's slipper lay. If he did indeed find Ellia, how would she greet him? How would he greet her? Every part of his body seemed to ache to hold his little lass…yet she wasn't little anymore. She would be almost a woman.

The carriage stopped. Raoul's heartbeat quickened as Jolin opened the door. They walked past a dozen cottages before Raoul broke the silence. "You know you can find Nes's abode without asking?"

"Aye. Galien gave clear instructions. Are you certain you are calm enough to face Nes?"

Raoul nodded, though the very mention of the man's name made his blood boil. He took a deep breath and nodded again.

"Mayhap I should go first."

Raoul frowned at Jolin. "I am capable of controlling myself."

Jolin looked doubtful as he strode up the lane.

Intolerable man. Raoul jogged a few steps to catch up with him as Jolin crossed into another lane.

At the third cottage, Jolin stopped. His powerful fist thundered on the door. No answer. Raoul's throat went dry. Even if he wanted to shout a threat toward Nes, he couldn't have. Again, Jolin knocked.

"If ye're lookin' fer the man, he died."

Jolin and Raoul spun around. A wee lad about seven years old stared at them, his eyes wide and face solemn.

"He has feigned death before," Raoul muttered.

Jolin shook his head at Raoul and turned to the lad. "Died? When was this?"

The lad shrugged. "I know not exactly. It was after he had a visitor."

"A visitor?"

"Aye. My father found him kilt." The lad shuddered. "Does a man have to be cruel to have enemies?"

Raoul's heart went out to him as Jolin's voice lowered with compassion. "You needn't worry of acquiring enemies."

The frown on the lad's face lifted. "I don't want enemies like he had." He bowed slightly and turned.

"You're not going to press further?" Raoul asked Jolin.

Jolin shook his head. "Can you not see the lad is disturbed? We may ask others to verify the statement."

Raoul looked back at the cottage. "It had to have been Bioti." He had to find her before she laid hands on his daughter. He raised his voice. "Lad, may we speak with your father?"

"Aye, he is at home." The lad continued his walk.

Raoul rubbed his hands together as he followed the lad. If the lad's father had found Nes, mayhap he knew him and his acquaintances. One could hope, at the least.

Jolin didn't speak as they followed the lad into his cottage.

"Men to speak with you, Father."

A man around Raoul's age stood and bowed. "To whom do I owe this honor?"

"Lord Kiralyn," Jolin introduced.

The man bowed again. "Reynold, at your service."

"I came seeking Nes," Raoul said.

Reynold frowned. "I hope your need of him was not of importance."

"Aye, of great importance."

"I am sorry, then. He died yestermorn."

"I thought your lad said he was kilt."

Reynold nodded as he crossed his arms. "'Twas the cause of his death. His attacker must have thought him dead when he left."

"Before he died…did he say anything of importance?"

Jolin placed a hand on Raoul's arm. Raoul gritted his teeth. Of course. How was the stranger to know what information he needed?

"Do you know who attacked him?" Jolin asked.

"Nay."

"Did he mention any names?"

"The man could scarcely breathe." Reynold narrowed his eyes. "Of what matter would it be to you?"

It would be impossible to work with this man. Raoul took a step toward the door.

"One last question," Jolin said, "then we shall leave."

Reynold waited.

"Was there a place that Nes frequented apart from home?"

"If ye're looking for family, he had none."

"Aye, we know. Yet you did not answer my question. Have you ever known Nes to frequent Abtshire?"

Reynold sighed and rubbed his face. "I suppose it makes no difference. Of late, I have heard of him speaking of trips to Abtshire. I know not why."

"Thank you." Jolin turned to Raoul and motioned him to follow him out the door.

"Abtshire?" Raoul whispered as the door closed behind them.

Jolin gave him a half-grin.

"How did you know?"

"Merely a suspicion, m'lord."

Whatever those suspicions, it was time to act, and quickly.

Chapter Twelve

Outside of Abtshire

"Can you not go faster?" Bioti hissed.

Lia used one hand to steady herself, the other to keep hold of the reins. "We would go faster, had we taken the king's highway."

"Lower your voice, child! We are not going the direction of the king's highway."

"Nay, we are running. From what, pray tell? From your visitor?" Her stomach knotted as she said the words. She would give anything to know from whom Bioti was running. Whoever it was must be more terrifying than the sheriff, to lead her to steal from the man.

Bioti boxed Lia's ear, making her jerk the reins. Hauch slowed.

"Focus on your driving."

Lia sat up and urged Hauch forward, her heart pounding faster than the beat of Hauch's hooves. *And just what would you do if I did stop the horse—and let Sheriff Feroci find you?* She didn't dare say the words aloud. If there were some way for her to report Bioti's theft, she would. But if she went on foot, Bioti would be miles away before she could find someone who trusted her word. *I don't want to be here! I don't want to be your thief.* Thief. She shuddered at the word. She didn't have a choice. There was no one in all of Abtshire to whom she could flee. *Except Dumphey and Noel.* She pushed the thought aside. It was too late now.

The moon hid behind the trees, making the pathway hard to find. Geva and Helga moaned as the cart jolted. All because of Lia's poor driving, Bioti would say.

She had to find a way out of this. Lia stared at Hauch's broad back. If she could convince Bioti and her daughters to step off and lighten the load… Nay, they wouldn't fall for such a prank. If they stopped to rest… Lia glanced sideways at Bioti. The woman was staring ahead, her eyes wide—whether from fear of what lay in these forests or fear of who may follow them, Lia didn't know. Bioti would never agree to stop.

Why me? The question plagued Lia. First, she was born with a deformed foot, then placed in the care of someone like Bioti.

Bioti looked behind her then shoved Lia aside and grabbed the reins. Lia gripped the side of the cart, keeping herself from toppling over.

"You are slow at everything, child!" She slapped the leather over Hauch's back. The horse picked up speed.

Lia gripped the seat with both hands as she looked behind her. A few specs of light flickered in the distance. Highwaymen? The sheriff's men? There was no way to know at this distance.

The moaning from Geva and Helga grew louder.

"Hush, daughters, or it shall be the end of you!"

Geva made some comment, but the rumbling of the wheels covered it up.

"Where are they now?" Bioti whispered.

Lia glanced behind. The lights were larger. "Closer." Her heart began pounding, harder than when she had stolen Hauch.

"How close?" Bioti's voice rose in pitch.

"See for yourself." Lia didn't want to risk losing her grip on the wagon.

Bioti turned then muttered a curse as she pulled on the reins.

"What are we doing?" Lia asked, keeping her voice low.

"*We* are doing nothing." Bioti threw the reins into Lia's lap. "Helga, Geva, off quickly." She hopped down from the cart then looked up at Lia. "You, keep going and do not stop."

"But what if the men attack me?"

Bioti placed a hand on each of her daughters. "Then you didn't heed my warning." She stepped up to the cart and grabbed Lia. "You are out here alone. Make sure they understand that. Alone."

She led her daughters into the shadowy forest. Lia tore her eyes away from Bioti's retreating form and glanced back. Her throat went dry.

Chapter Thirteen

Abtshire

Not a word passed between Jolin and Raoul as they galloped down the road. The hoof beats of his hired horse seemed to chant, "Pray… Pray… Pray!"

I tried. Raoul's hands were clammy where they gripped the reins. *God, I have sought Thee.* Hadn't he? He silenced his conscience. His prayers had throbbed with, "Let me find her," or other demands. That was prayer, was it not?

The silhouette of Abtshire rose in front of them. Jolin pulled his horse to a stop behind Raoul.

"Why are you stopping?" Raoul reined in even as he asked.

"What is our plan, m'lord?"

"Discover where Bioti is hiding."

Jolin sniffed. “No one will open their doors to a stranger at midnight, unless he has an order from the king.”

Raoul shook his head. He wasn’t going to beg interference of his brother. “No sense in turning back tonight.” He heeled his horse to a walk.

“Mayhap. But you need a plan.”

Raoul let out a frustrated sigh. *Pray. Really pray.* That was what Elayne would suggest, and rightfully so. *God hasn’t given me answers yet; just more questions and problems. Sometimes one needs to find the answers for themselves. God gave us a brain, not only prayer.* Why did he fight against the thought of praying yet again?

Before he could figure out the answer, they were entering the streets of Abtshire. Jolin stopped his horse in front of a cottage. The windows were dark, like the rest of the cottages on the road. Raoul dismounted and walked to the door.

“I think it unwise, Raoul.”

Raoul gritted his teeth. “When did I give permission to use my given name?”

“It hasn’t bothered you before. I beg pardon, m’lord.” His apology sounded insincere.

Raoul clenched his fists, but shoved them into his pockets rather than knock on the door. He turned as the watchman approached.

“May I help you?” the watchman asked.

"Aye," Jolin said. "We would like a room for the night."

"The Lyre Inn is on the other side of town. You must be strangers in Abtshire."

"Aye," Raoul said. The man needed no explanation.

"One last thing," Jolin said as the watchman turned. "Know you of a woman named Bioti?"

Raoul could have pummeled Jolin. The man kept his own rules, forbidding his lord to do one thing, and then taking his own initiative in another.

"She's not here."

Not here? Did that mean…

"But she *was* here?" Raoul asked, keeping eagerness from lacing his voice.

"Aye."

"You are certain?"

"M'lord, surely there is more than one Bioti," Jolin reasoned.

Raoul ground his teeth. Confounded man. His words dashed out Raoul's hope like a bucket of cold water on wee embers just taking spark.

"Tell us of this Bioti," Raoul said, forcing the words through clenched teeth.

The watchman settled his bobbing lantern and gestured with his hands. "She was about this height, brown hair, harsh face. Well, all of her was harsh, really. She didn't talk much. Kept to herself."

The description was close enough. Raoul felt hope rise again.

"She up and left. Probably fleeing the sheriff's pay, but he'll catch her. Or whoever stole his cart. He doesn't let anyone get away from him." He started walking away. "Take the main road to the other end of town. You'll find the inn."

"Wait!" Raoul ran after the man. "Did Bioti have any children? Daughters?" He could feel desperation growing in his voice.

"Aye."

"How many?"

The man raised his lantern until it blinded Raoul. "Why should you need to know?"

Bury these men who wouldn't trust a stranger with basic information. "'Tis a matter of…importance." Something kept Raoul from disclosing his daughter's assumed kidnapping to a stranger, even if it was a town's watchman.

"Well, you came a day too late."

"They left yesterday?"

"Close to it. A few hours ago."

"Which way did they go?"

The watchman shook his head as he lowered his lantern. "I've said all that I'm telling you."

"I am Lord Kiralyn—"

"Then you must speak to Sheriff Feroci or Lord Trey."

Raoul ground his teeth as he spun on his heel and went back to Jolin. “Did you suspect she was here?”

“Only since talking with Reynold. No hard facts, though. Merely suspicion.”

“You should inform me even of suspicions.”

In the dim light, Raoul could see Jolin raise his eyebrows as if in surprise. Then, his face changed to something Raoul couldn’t quite read. “If my suspicions never turn into hard facts, then the last thing I want is to worry you into borrowing trouble.”

Raoul clamped his mouth shut before he spewed hateful words at his friend.

“Come, m’lord, we shall rest, then search in the morn.”

Chapter Fourteen

Outside of Abtshire

Lia's whole body trembled as she slapped the reins on Hauch. He seemed to sense her desperation and hurried from walk to trot. It still was not fast enough. Every time she looked back, the torches shone bigger. The wagon lurched, throwing her to one side.

"Halt in the name of the king!"

Highway men? Likely not. Which made Lia shake harder. Even if she had stopped the cart when Bioti fled, she would never have gotten away through the tangled briars that snaked through the forest floor. Bioti knew that. A sickening knot tightened in Lia's stomach.

Torches flashed past. Horsemen surrounded her. The cart stopped.

Lia clenched her hands over the reins and bowed her head, squeezing her eyes shut. If they were going to kill her here, she didn't want to see it coming.

"Lia?"

She jerked her head up, looking into Dumphey's face, filled with shock.

"What have you done?"

"'Twasn't me!" Lia's heart pounded. "I promise!"

Men moved past Dumphey. Rough hands pulled Lia out of the cart. Their grip tightened as her feet hit the ground.

"You know her?"

"Aye." Dumphey glanced at the men. "She can't run away. You needn't hold her thus."

The grip loosened, making Lia's stomach lurch. It wasn't that Dumphey trusted her to *not* run away. He knew she couldn't. Tears filled Lia's eyes as she looked up at him. "'Twas Bioti! She ordered me to steal the horse—"

"You cannot blame her for your part in this." Dumphey avoided her gaze as he muttered the words.

"She is in these woods. She made me stop and drop her off when she saw you coming. I can point where they got off." Lia tried to raise her hand, but the men's grip kept her arms pinned to her sides.

"Did you seriously think you could get away with this, Lia?" Dumphey's voice was low.

"I didn't want to. Bioti…you must find—"

"Silence!" The harsh order was given by someone other than Dumphey.

Lia bit her tongue as tears streamed down her cheeks.

"You do not have orders to question her," the man said to Dumphey, "but to track the thief."

Dumphey's glance toward Lia only sent the tears flowing faster. Then he turned his back to her.

The leader glared at Lia. "We will let the sheriff deal with you."

The men holding Lia lifted her. This time, to toss her in the back of the cart.

"You there. Drive."

Through her tears, Lia watched as Dumphey obeyed without a word. His shoulders slumped as he pulled the reins into his hands. The other men surrounded the cart, their torches flickering as thunder echoed through the air.

Lia huddled among the goods in the cart. The night temperature dropped as the wind began blowing harder. Life was unfair. Bioti could do one evil thing after another and get away with it, the blame always falling on Lia's shoulders. Even Dumphey didn't trust her, no matter how kind he had been to her. That was Bioti's fault too. The woman had made her life miserable, torn her away from any friends she might have.

The tears didn't stop their steady stream for the whole ride back to Abtshire. The cart stopped in front of Sheriff Feroci's home and someone pounded on his door.

"Dumphey." Lia's voice was hoarse. The lad didn't so much as move a muscle. "Dumphey, what are they going to do with me?"

"They oughta hang ye, like all thieves deserve!" The severe voice wasn't Dumphey's.

"Is it true?" Lia whispered. She reached out until her fingers brushed against Dumphey. His shoulders rose and fell. Somehow, she knew that was the only answer he would give her.

"A pretty thief, eh?" Sheriff Feroci walked up to the cart and looked in.

"Sir, I know you have no reason to believe me—"

"Eh, pretty enough for the dungeon. I don't have time to deal with her tonight." Feroci motioned to his men.

Once again, Lia was forced from the cart. The men seemed to easily drag her along, keeping her from using her feet. She willed the tears to stop flowing, but they only came faster as she was pulled to the dungeon.

She glanced back before they entered. Dumphey still sat motionless on the cart. He wouldn't help her.

No one would.

Chapter Fifteen

Abtshire

One candle flickered its dim light at the desk. Jolin's breathing rose and fell evenly, as it had the past hour or two. Raoul had been standing in front of the desk since Jolin lay down. His servant-friend had set Raoul's Bible on the desk. It was a task he always did, yet tonight, he had seemed to do it more…meaningfully? He hadn't said a word to Raoul, but he didn't need to.

Raoul knew he needed to open the Scriptures, to read them like he had neglected to do the past few days, but something held him back.

He made his way back to the window and looked over the streets of Abtshire. There wasn't much to see on this end of town. Sheriff Feroci's home was in the hustle of town, not here on the outskirts. A few public places, a cottage or two. Everything was silent and dark.

He stood still, his thumb and forefinger caressing his stubbled chin. "Lord, I want to find her." The same words had echoed in his mind over and over, never changing. "I have to find her. And soon." His lips moved, though no words came out.

Raoul shifted his gaze from the empty streets to the sky. Clouds overtook the midnight palette, refusing to let the moon through their density. Only a few stars peeked out in gaps left by the clouds. The heavy painting above him was a completely different picture than the night before, where stars sparkled as far as the eye could see.

When I consider Thy heavens, the work of Thy fingers, the moon and the stars, which Thou hast ordained;

The words flowed through his mind—the first portion of Bible he had allowed himself to meditate on in his search.

What is man, that Thou art mindful of him?

Raoul swallowed. He hadn't been spending the last few days telling God what he wanted…had he? Pride. That was what held him back from truly seeking and listening to God. He pressed his head against the window, listening as the rain started to pelt against it.

"Father, I'm sorry." The words seemed so shallow, yet it was where he needed to begin anew. He walked back to the desk, this time sitting down. He laid a hand on his Bible, the smooth leather sending him comfort. Not as much comfort as he knew the words inside held. He opened it, letting the pages flutter open. *Proverbs.* That was where one went for wisdom, was it not?

Trust in the Lord with all thine heart;

In his frantic haste to find Ellia, had he trusted in the Lord with *all* of his heart? Was not Ellia a part of his heart? Did he truly trust the Lord with her, even though he knew not of her whereabouts?

And lean not unto thine own understanding.

Raoul's eyes closed. Mayhap he did not know what was best in the search for his daughter. When all paths led to a dead end, he didn't know which way was right—according to his own understanding. But didn't this verse mean that following God required trusting Him, even when one could not see the path ahead? Raoul opened his eyes again. Though he knew the passage by heart, seeing the words printed on the page made the message sink in.

In all thy ways acknowledge Him, and He shall direct thy paths.

How had he acknowledged God these past days? He hadn't. That was the simple truth. Should he wonder, then, why it seemed as if God's direction was silent?

Raoul sank to the floor, onto his knees. "Father above, I beseech Thee for Thy forgiveness." He curled his fingers into a fist. "Thou seest how greatly I desire to be reunited with my daughter again. I want her safely here. More now than ever. But, Lord, I realize I need to be surrendered to Thee." His fists clenched tighter, his fingernails slicing into his palms. "Help me to surrender." Gradually his fists loosened. He bowed his head lower and reached his arms in front of him, hands open wide. "Thy will be done."

Chapter Sixteen

Abtshire

Lia hugged her knees to her chest, willing her body to stop shaking. It was because it was cold down here. Not because she was afraid. Her eyes wouldn't adjust to the darkness. *Down in the dungeon.* Her teeth chattered. Mayhap she was scared.

Chains rustled. Lia froze.

"Newcomer, eh?"

Even if she tried, Lia wasn't sure she could speak.

"A wee lass? What evil did you do?" There was a hint of pity in this stranger's voice.

Lia swallowed back the tears. *'Twasn't my evil!* Mayhap the stranger would believe her. If only she could form her thoughts into words.

"Ye best get some sleep." The voice sounded motherly. Or grandmotherly, given the huskiness.

Sleep? In this place? And with iron pressing against her ankles?

"Though…if ye were not to sleep, a soul gets a mite lonesome down here. Can ye talk, lass?"

Lia heard a whimper. Had it come from her? She opened her mouth, but her "aye" skittered through the shadows like dust.

"Well, mayhap ye can give a listen. I've been having a right jolly time down here."

"J-jolly?" Lia's voice squeaked as if it were a rusty gate, not wanting to let her voice out.

"Aha! She does speak." The hoarse voice laughed. "My name is Zuzene. I don't get much company nowadays besides the rodents. But the good Father above doesn't mind that. It gives Him and me more time to speak."

Surely time alone had made this woman go daft. Lia shuddered. "How…how long have you been…down here?"

"I lose count. Some days, I wish Feroci would just give up past offenses and release me. Other days, I wish he'd get so angry he'd kill me."

"That is awful!" Lia shuddered again. Then, she realized that her uncontrollable shaking had ceased. Or, at least had lessened.

"I have frightened you, lass." Zuzene's voice turned gentle. "Too eager for company, I suppose. What is your name?"

"Lia."

"Lia." Zuzene rolled the name off her tongue as if she were a child tasting a confection. "Tell me about yourself, Lia."

"'Tisn't much to tell." The days of the past molded together to form a lump of dark, meaningless nothing.

"Surely there is."

"I am a cripple." There. The words that had refused to flee her lips were uttered in the safety of darkness.

"A cripple? And that makes nothing much to tell? How did you become a cripple?"

"I know not." Lia's brain was foggy or she would try to redirect the conversation.

"Is that why you are here?"

"Nay." Lia caught her breath. "Aye!" Was that not why she was here? Because she couldn't run away—not from Bioti, not from the sheriff's men.

"Poor lass. Mayhap a night of sleep will clear the confusion."

"A night's sleep will not keep me from death." As she said the word, a vice grip seemed to tighten around her throat. *Death!* It seemed to bounce around the underground walls.

"You are certain of death?"

"Whyever not? Is that not the sheriff's penalty for stealing—if there is no way to prove innocence?"

"Ah." Zuzene drew the word out, long and breathy.

"In that case, we have all night. I will listen if you care to share about it."

Lia hesitated. She had nothing more to lose. Mayhap talking it out would ease her confusion. Give an answer to her problem. She took a shuddering breath and began talking about the one whose fault she was here: Bioti. When she finished, with how Bioti's wile had landed her in the dungeon, Zuzene clicked her tongue.

"This Bioti. She sounds like she is miserable."

"Her? Miserable?" Lia laughed. An empty shell of a laugh.

"Ye think not?"

Lia stretched her legs, wincing as the iron grated against the stone floor. "I try not to give more thought to Bioti than necessary."

"Aye, 'twas what I thought." Deep sympathy laced Zuzene's voice. Sympathy for Lia or…for Bioti?

"What of you?" Lia was tired of hearing how her voice echoed around the room, sounding small and fearful. "You have asked my story. Now tell me yours."

"Eh, 'tisn't much to tell. I lived in a cottage above here. I angered someone, some of which was my own doing, and was cast down here."

"Yet not killed?"

"Nay." Zuzene chuckled. "He doesn't hate me enough to kill me. That would torment his conscience. As long as I am alive and fed, he has me out of sight and thinks he can live peaceably."

"Who?" Lia's mind spun around Zuzene's first words. "The sheriff?"

"Mayhap. It doesn't matter at any rate. I have forgiven him."

"Even if it was not all your fault?"

"Well, I could rust down here in bitterness. Which, I suppose, would make me as miserable as your Bioti."

Lia rubbed her legs where the chills had begun again. This time, she was certain it was from the dampness of underground.

"So tell me, Lia…what if they did come for you on the morrow, and you were to die? Are you ready for that?"

The shivers started again. More violent this time. "I… 'twould be just as well for me. My life here has been miserable." Bioti had seen to that.

"Why would you say that? Every one of God's creations has a beautiful purpose."

Lia choked on another piece of hollow laughter. 'Twas the dungeon's fault. She wasn't usually this cynical. "If He had a purpose for me, He would have made me beautiful to make up for my limp. Or, if I were to be ugly, then at least He could have given me two good feet."

"You think God didn't love you, and has cursed you?"

That was a good enough explanation.

"Lia, all of God's creations are fearfully and wonderfully made. Beauty is not about what a person looks like, but about who a person is."

"A slave to Bioti. That makes me beautiful?" Lia spat the words out. She didn't believe them for one moment. "Such love to make one's childhood nothing but a nightmare."

"But God didn't do that."

"What did He do then?" Lia folded her arms in front of her and leaned against the wall. It was probably mildewed and filthy, but it wasn't like her dress was a gown.

"He sent His Son to die for you. To take away your sins." There was a smile in Zuzene's voice. "Yes, He made us all fearfully and wonderfully. Yes, He loves us. But we are all sinners. You could be the most beautiful lass in the shire, but if you died without accepting His salvation, that beauty would do no good. Your *heart* must be made beautiful. And that can only happen by believing on the Lord Jesus Christ for salvation."

When did the conversation turn from her life to God? Lia closed her eyes. Her head felt heavy. If she could only sleep…nay, that would bring her closer to the dawn of death. A wave of chills washed over her. She would listen to Zuzene talk. It distracted her from the coming doom.

Chapter Seventeen

Abtshire

The hours of the morn had dragged out, yet not as the past few days had. The weight from Raoul's chest had lifted, and sometime in the night, his head had stopped throbbing.

He had dressed in common garb to blend in without suspicion and was now watching the townspeople as they milled around. Women with their baskets, men with their tools. Had it been yesterday, he would have stopped every single one of them, inquiring after Bioti. Today, he chose his subjects cautiously.

A man rode through town on horseback, the people moving to make way for the horse. The chestnut hung his head low as he plodded. The horse needed rest. Raoul glanced up at the rider.

"Galien!"

Galien jerked his head toward Raoul. "M'lord…" He jumped off his horse and walked up to Raoul, his fair skin flushed red from the quick exertion. "I thought you were going to Fordyce."

"So we did," Raoul said. "What finds you here?" He hadn't thought to send word concerning his whereabouts. He grimaced. He needed to send a note to Elayne. She would be worried, even though she knew of his search.

"I remembered Nes mentioning Abtshire. I thought, mayhap I could investigate here and bring you news. I see you have preceded me." Galien fidgeted with the reins of his horse.

Jolin joined them. "I see we have reinforcement. Have you been here long enough to ask after Bioti?"

"She left," Galien said. "I haven't been here long."

"Aye, this we know," Jolin said. "Any idea as to her whereabouts?"

"Nes didn't say?"

Raoul shifted and cleared his throat. "Nes was dead."

Galien nodded and sighed. "'Twas for the best."

Jolin's brows furrowed. "What do you mean?"

Galien straightened. "He was an old man. Miserable."

"He was killed." Jolin's voice was flat. Suppressing outrage at Galien's insensitivity, Raoul knew.

Galien bowed his head slightly. "I am sorry to hear." He looked up at Raoul. "What are the plans now, m'lord? Have you any leads?"

Raoul sighed. "It appears everyone knows Bioti, but no one knows her whereabouts." He paused. It wasn't that the townspeople didn't want to speak of her. They truly didn't know.

"Mayhap the lass is not with her."

"No," Jolin said. "She's with her."

Raoul turned to look at him. "The watchman didn't disclose that."

Jolin shrugged, but Raoul knew that look. Jolin was hiding a smirk behind his serious façade. "I asked after her daughters. She has three. Or so people assume."

Raoul's hands felt clammy. He wiped them on his pants. "That much we already know."

"Aye," Jolin agreed. "But I have names. Helga, Geva..." He paused, his blue eyes turning serious. "And a lass they call Lia."

Raoul forced air into his lungs. Lia was close enough to Ellia, was it not? But then, wouldn't Bioti have changed her name entirely? *She had no reason to; she thought I wouldn't find out.*

"Do you believe Nes told Bioti of our search?" Jolin asked.

"And then she killed him before running?" The headache was returning. Raoul massaged his temples as the noise of the street seemed to rise. It seemed to make sense.

"Bioti? A murderer?" Galien's voice was too loud to be in the middle of a crowded street. Raoul glared at him.

"We haven't proof." Jolin's soft voice seemed to counter the turmoil going on inside Raoul.

"If Bioti would do such to a man—"

Jolin frowned at Galien, stopping him from continuing. Raoul didn't need Galien to word his fears. A chill ran through his body as his mind began surmising. His hand slipped into his pocket. The silk of Ellia's slipper was smooth against his rough fingers. How would he face whatever the future held—for him, and for her? Comfort seemed as far away as the hope of finding his daughter.

Trust in the Lord.

Aye, that was how he would face the answer.

The wind blew in short puffs, threading its invisible fingers through Raoul's hair as he walked through the center of Abtshire, where Jolin and Galien had agreed to meet him midday. Though he knew it was unlikely that Ellia was in the crowded streets, he couldn't keep from observing each lass's gait. They all skipped or walked steadily as they did their tasks. Which was a good thing, unless one was looking for a lass who was unable to do either. Surely, in the years gone by, Ellia's limp would be noticeable to any passerby. The physicians had warned Raoul that, if not tended to properly, Ellia could end up a cripple by her twenties. Raoul rolled his shoulders and straightened. Why did these memories come unburied with news that Ellia hadn't died? How crippled would she be, not having the physician's care that she would have if she had stayed with Raoul?

"May I help you, sir?" A lad stepped forward, lugging two buckets of water.

"Nay, I am only waiting for someone. Thank you."

The lad nodded. "Very well." He continued toward the stables, the weight of the buckets not slowing him down.

Only waiting. The words pounded in Raoul's head as he glanced around. Galien appeared in the distance, but he stopped to talk with a man several paces away. His back was to Raoul, as he reached for his pouch. Drawing something out, he handed it to the man, then they continued to talk, the man giving gestures. Raoul frowned. Before they parted ways this morn, he hadn't provided the men with bribe money.

Gratitude swelled in Raoul's heart. It would be just like Galien to use his own coins to help, not waiting to locate Raoul for the money. He would have to address the matter later and repay Galien.

After talking with the man, Galien slipped off again. Raoul crossed his arms. Hadn't they agreed to meet soon—or if they found a lead?

Raoul slipped through the crowds, his focus on Galien's uncapped blond head. He was moving swiftly, with purpose. Raoul checked the excitement growing inside of him. Galien was quicker to jump to suppositions than Jolin. If Jolin were going through the streets at that pace, he was sure to be on something. Galien? There was only one way to find out.

The crowd congested in front of Raoul. He stopped and stood on his toes, but Galien was nowhere to be seen. He shoved forward, pushing the commoners back to clear his way. At the end of the crowd, Raoul looked around. A fist seemed to tighten around his heart. *'Twas just Galien. He'll tell me later.* But he didn't want to wait until later for news.

The brown-headed lad from earlier stepped in his path, his eyes looking heavenward, as if following the flight of a bird.

"Have you seen a blond man come through here?"

"Is he the man for whom you were waiting?"

"One of them, aye."

"Is he in trouble?"

Raoul shook his head and let out an exasperated sigh. "Nay." Why were the townspeople so careful with their tongues?

"Do you know the man?" The lad set his empty buckets on the ground as he rubbed his hands together. They were red from the coarse hemp rope.

"Why would I be asking you about the man, if I knew him not?"

The lad shrugged and picked up his buckets again.

"What is your name?" Raoul wasn't going to let this opportunity slip past. "How long have you lived here?" They hadn't started on the best grounds for conversation and information-passing, but it was worth a try.

"Noel. I was born and raised in this village." A glimmer of pride shone in his brown eyes.

"Then you know everyone in the village?" Raoul asked. "My men and I are on the search for someone."

Noel looked wary. He was a smart lad for his young age. "Who is it you want to know of?"

"A woman named Bioti and her daughters, Geva, Helga, and…" Raoul caught himself before Ellia's real name slipped out. "Lia." The two-syllable name felt strange on his tongue.

Something flashed through Noel's face, then it was as if a mask slid in place. "What do you wish to know of them?"

"She has…she was living in this village, was she not? It is needful for me to find her, before she…harms someone I know."

Noel lifted his chin as he moved forward. "Why don't you ask your man? He's spoken with this Bioti you're looking for."

"Galien? Today?" Raoul put a hand out to stop the lad as he thought back to the person Galien met in the middle of town. It hadn't been Bioti. "What do you mean?" He could hear his voice harden as he asked the question.

Noel looked up with a frown. "Whose side are you on? Bioti's?"

"Nay!" The word exploded from Raoul's lips. How could even a stranger who knew Bioti wonder if he was on her side? Yet, if Galien had been seen with Bioti...

"I…" Raoul looked at the lad's doubtful eyes. *Father, I need to know who I can trust.* Placed in the wrong hands, news of the lord's daughter being alive could be dangerous. He took a breath and peace calmed him. "I care about Lia. If I can find Bioti, Lia will be safe. I will personally see to it."

Noel's eyes widened and his fingers released the buckets. "You can give your word?"

Raoul's heart rate quickened. Was Ellia in danger? What other information could Noel give of her whereabouts? Raoul had to stay with what Noel was willing to give, though. "Aye, I give my word." He lowered his voice. Somehow, he knew Noel needed to know his identity. "I am Lord Kiralyn. Bioti has wronged me and I fear that her heart is bent on evil."

Noel raised his eyebrows as he surveyed Raoul's clothes then dipped in respect.

"Treat me no differently," Raoul warned as he noticed Noel about to speak.

Noel nodded, stopped to pick up his buckets, then motioned for Raoul to follow him to the well in the center of town. "If it will help Lia, I'll see what I can do." The lad's voice was low, but he spoke quickly. "There is only one person I know who would know of Bioti's whereabouts."

"Take me to him," Raoul said.

Noel shook his head as he filled his buckets with water from the well. "She is in the dungeon. No visitors allowed." He looked up at Raoul and his brownish-blond locks fell over his forehead. He pushed them back, revealing his eyes, shining honest and trustworthy. "I bring their food. She is to hang…" His eyes clouded. "I will try my best to ask for information." He retrieved his buckets and disappeared into the crowd.

Chapter Eighteen

Abtshire

A shaft of light pierced through the darkness, growing as the door was pushed open.

"Breakfast for two." The bearer's voice was young, joyful, and…familiar.

Lia shaded her eyes as the lad walked closer.

"Here you are, madam. I managed to slip in a fresh apple."

"You naughty lad." A smile belied Zuzene's reprimand. She reached her hand out for the tray that was handed to her.

"And for you, Lia." The voice changed. More grim.

Lia reached out her hands for the tray, blinking as the rays continued to blind her.

"I have but one minute to stay, so talk fast."

"Nay, you talk fast." Lia's eyes finally adjusted so she could see Noel's features. "When am I to die?"

Noel stepped back. "Lia...do you know Bioti's destination?"

"Nay. She didn't say. Just...left." She studied Noel's face. "You didn't answer me."

Noel shook his head. "Eat up. You will need your strength." What kind of an answer was that?

"Noel!"

The lad stepped back into the blinding light. "If I tarry, I shall be punished." The door slammed shut, cloaking the dungeon in darkness.

How did he expect her to eat after that exchange? Mayhap he didn't truly want her to eat, but wanted to punish her. Her fingers found the tray of food. Dry bread. Her throat constricted. Prisoners' fare. No fresh apple for her. She touched a metal cup. The least she could manage was to ease her thirst from the long night. She emptied the cup and placed it back on the tray.

"Aren't you going to eat?" Zuzene asked.

Lia pushed the tray toward her. "I'm not hungry."

"You are worried."

To deny it would be a lie that Zuzene could see straight through.

"Lia, whatever is going to happen, you must turn to Christ. Whether it is to live down here a decade or die today, His grace will see you through."

Lia curled into a ball, fighting against the shivers that pulsed through her body. She wasn't sure she was ready to do that. She just wanted everything to stop—the pain, the turmoil, the confusion, the injustice.

The lock in the door turned. If it were possible, Lia's stomach did a complete flip. Their breakfast had been brought. There was no other reason for an intrusion, unless it was to bring her to her death.

"Lia."

She recognized the soft voice as Dumphey's.

The door closed again. Steady footsteps walked forward and stopped before her. Given the rustle of clothes, Dumphey must have knelt down.

Lia couldn't look at him, illuminated by the candle he held. Instead, she studied the cracks in the wall, caked with mud. How long had this place been here? And where did that thought come from?

"Lia, you must tell me. Where is Bioti?"

"I know not." She couldn't make herself speak louder than a murmur.

"Lia." The light shifted upwards and Dumphey shook her. "This is the last way I could save you—you must tell me."

"I know not!" A single sob ripped from Lia's chest. "If I knew, I would have told Noel." She turned to him, reading sorrow in his face. "Trust me, Dumphey. You must."

Dumphey groaned and leaned back on his heels. "'Tis injustice." His voice was low. "Yet I know not what to do."

Lia sat up. "They really will hang me?" She wasn't sure the words reached Dumphey, they felt so light and airy.

"In the sheriff's eyes, all evidence points to you—"

"But you believe I didn't do it."

Dumphey looked away. "Bioti and her daughters are missing, but Sheriff Feroci refuses to send a search party."

"The horse and cart are returned. Is that not enough? He could simply let me rot down here!"

"You know he's the law." Why did Dumphey have to say it so gravely?

The chills turned into sobs. Chains rustled then rough arms wrapped around her. Zuzene's voice droned nearby, in her ear. Comforting her, reprimanding Dumphey, then saying nothing at all. It must have been her gentle hand that caressed Lia's tangled hair as Lia fought away the tears. Finally, all was still.

"There, there…" Zuzene's voice hummed low, like a faraway memory of a lullaby. If only she could add words of comfort, to tell Lia that Dumphey was lying. But Lia knew she wouldn't. If Zuzene had spoken anything in the few hours she'd known her, it was the truth.

"Lia, I—"

"Dumphey," Zuzene interrupted his soft voice. "I think you have said enough. I'll care for her. Go along, do what you can. And if anything happens, you need not blame yourself."

Blame himself? Through her tears, Lia watched as Dumphey and the light disappeared back through the door. How well did Zuzene know these lads? She blinked back her tears. That was not of any importance when she stood at death's door.

Zuzene's hand slowed. "Death is not a frightful thing if you know the One to Whom you'll go."

"I don't." Even heaven wouldn't accept a deformed outcast like her.

"Have you thought on what I said last night?"

Nay, she had blocked out as many words as she could. This was not her last day of living. It couldn't be!

"Lia." Zuzene placed a hand on each of Lia's shoulders. "I cannot force you to accept Jesus Christ, and neither does He. Yet I can guarantee you that He wants you to come. He is not willing for any to perish, but that all should come to repentance."

"Then why an early death?" It seemed a fitting end to her life: injustice coming on the tail of slavery and pain.

"I haven't an answer for that, but I can point you to the One Who knows all."

Lia's shoulders fell. Whatever was left of her broken life, it wouldn't hurt to listen to what Zuzene had to say.

"Things in this world will never be fair, as long as men and women do not love God. But life isn't about today or even about tomorrow. Life is about eternity. When God created the world, I believe He intended for us all to live with Him eternally. But sin entered into the world. And with sin, came death and separation from God."

Aye, she felt the pain of both death and separation.

"I am just as much a sinner as you…or Bioti, or the sheriff. When it comes to God's eyes, we are all equal. Either we are lost sinners or redeemed sinners. The difference comes by whether or not we accept Christ's gift of salvation—which He has freely offered to all of us."

"What sin did I commit to be born a cripple?" Lia asked, cynicism again creeping into her voice.

"Ah, Jesus was asked a similar question when He was on earth. A man was born blind, and everyone wondered who had sinned: him or his parents? Jesus Himself said that it was neither, but that this man was born blind so that men could see the glory of God. Jesus healed him and made him see. But greater than that, this man believed that Jesus is the Son of God and was saved. That was the greater healing."

Silence dropped between them for a moment, then Zuzene spoke again, "Lia, the question is not about the deformity of your body but about the deformity of your soul."

Lia's hand reached down to massage her foot, sending spasms of pain up her leg. She had learned ages ago that she couldn't hide her limp, but the many things she did strive to hide—bitterness, anger, unforgiveness—swarmed before her. Things that, considering what little she knew of God's righteousness, did not please Him. This was what separated her from God, and this is what Jesus Christ died for.

She would always be a cripple, but a choice dangled before her—a choice that, if she accepted, would allow her to limp to death as what Zuzene called a redeemed sinner.

"I think I want Jesus to cleanse my heart," she said, tears starting again. This time, they were not tears of fear.

Chapter Nineteen

Abtshire

"I thought we were to meet at noon," Jolin said. He had likely been waiting for a half hour.

Raoul grabbed Jolin's arm and led him away from the town center, where the townspeople were milling in thick clusters. "I need to speak with you privately. Have you seen Galien?"

"Nay…" Jolin gave Raoul a searching look as he matched Raoul's long stride. "He was supposed to meet us here as well."

"Yet he did not." Raoul didn't stop walking until they entered The Lyre Inn. He pushed the door of his room shut and leaned against the wall. The stiffness of it pressing his back made him aware of just how hard his heart was pounding. "I ran across a lad who says Galien talked with Bioti. Yet Bioti left days ago."

"You trust this lad?"

"I saw Galien pay a man for information."

"And…?"

Raoul scowled at Jolin. "I have heard nothing from him of the matter."

"You doubt Galien?"

Raoul leaned his head against the wall and shut his eyes. "I know not what to think." How could he explain it? Jolin hadn't talked with Noel nor seen his honesty as he had given Raoul his suspicions of Galien conversing with Bioti. In halted words, he shared those details with Jolin.

When Raoul opened his eyes again, Jolin had his hand on his chin, his blue eyes looking off into the distance. Raoul knew he was thinking through every aspect, pulling together details like only his mind could. Mayhap he could pull together something out of Raoul's confusion.

Jolin looked at Raoul, but the way his brows furrowed gave Raoul no encouragement.

"Noel says—"

The door opened and Galien entered. Raoul's body tensed, but Jolin's low soft voice indicated nothing as he asked, "Have you found any leads?"

Galien shook his head. "Nay. No one is willing to say anything."

"You were saying, m'lord?" Jolin's eyes warned Raoul against jumping to conclusions against Galien.

Raoul sighed. “Noel says there is only one friend who would know of Bioti’s destination, but she is a thief and will hang before the morrow.”

“Is there a way we could question her?” Jolin asked.

“Noel said no visitors are allowed. Unless I could somehow make a deal with Feroci and this prisoner…”

Jolin sniffed. “The man’s reputation is notorious.”

“And the prisoner a thief,” Galien pointed out. "Would you release a thief?”

There was nothing to reply. *Father, show me the way. It looks clouded again.*

Go.

The answer pressed itself inside Raoul’s heart. His fingers tightened into a ball. What would he say to Feroci when they met? His rank held little power in another lord’s realm, and he doubted King Jarin would get involved.

Go.

Raoul turned and placed a hand on the door.

“What are you doing?” Galien asked.

“I’m going.” The urge to do so quickly built pressure inside him. “You may follow if you desire.” He swung open the door and rushed outside.

A crowd had gathered on the opposite side of the village. If that was where the thief was to be hung, there wasn’t much time. Feroci must have changed his mind and ordered the hanging sooner. If Raoul didn’t have adequate time to speak with Feroci or the prisoner…

Lean not unto thine own understanding.

Raoul slowed to a walk as the crowd became denser. If this was not the way God intended him to find Ellia, He would make another way, if it was His will.

At the edge of the crowd, Raoul came to a full stop. He clambered onto a barrel and looked over the heads of the townspeople. On the other end, a man sat astride his horse. He must be the sheriff. If Raoul could weave around the people, he might have a chance to speak with Feroci…if the man would acknowledge him, dressed as a commoner. Bury propriety! He shouldn't have to bring robes everywhere he went.

A hush fell over the crowd. A man stood on the gallows, scroll in hand.

"Today, we give example of how the law tolerates thieves, be them old or young, male or female." His harsh voice snapped out the words as he looked over the crowd. "Bring the child here."

Child? Raoul's stomach cinched as he looked at where the crowd parted. Noel and another lad stood on either side of a lass, not even of age. The law didn't allow children to endure such punishment untried, he was certain.

"I should like to walk alone." The lass's voice rang over the silent crowd.

The lads stepped aside as the lass walked forward. Her gait hitched as she walked forward—probably due to nervous anticipation. But the next step was just as stilted. And the next.

Raoul leaned forward. Her face looked familiar. She was the same lass he had run into days before. The one whose eyes were filled with worry and turmoil.

Whispered voices fluttered through the crowd. "It's the cripple."

The cripple? Raoul snapped his focus back to the lass. She limped forward, her eyes filled with calm serenity, peace, and…

"Stop!" Raoul leapt off the barrel and shoved his way through the crowd, pushing people out of the way as he rushed forward.

The lass limped to the foot of the steps. She met the gaze of the man above.

Raoul dodged between two men. The lass was making her way up the steps. She pushed aside Noel, who had reached forward to offer assistance. She reached the top. The soldiers grabbed her and pulled her forward.

Raoul raced to the stairs.

"Stop him!" a husky voice snarled.

He was pulled back to the ground and seized by the guards.

A hood was slipped over the lass's head.

"Stop!" Raoul fought against the hand that held him. "In the name of King Jarin, I command you to stop."

That did nothing to appease the men holding him.

“Have we a madman afoot?” The smooth, rich voice thundered above him.

Raoul lifted his head to glare at Sheriff Feroci. “A madman I am not. If you would release me, I could prove I am the lord of Kiralyn.” He glared at the guards.

“This is not your province.”

“Nay, but the law of the land does not permit you to hang a child.” Raoul tore away from his captors and thrust his hand under Feroci’s nose. “Identify the seal.”

Feroci’s jaw ticked. “Do you demand the release of a thief who attempted to steal one of my finest horses and a cart full of goods?”

“I will repay anything that was damaged.”

“On what grounds?” Feroci glared at him.

Raoul met the glare with confidence. “She is my daughter.”

Chapter Twenty

Abtshire

His daughter? Lia struggled to turn around, to slip the hood off her head, but Feroci's man, Barat, kept a vice-grip on her. 'Twas impossible. Her father had died.

"Any man could claim that to save the life of a thief," Sheriff Feroci growled.

"Nay, I assure you. I have proof."

"The child has been in our village for years. What proof can you offer that she is daughter to a lord?"

The man fell silent. The daughter of a lord? Bless him for trying, but Lia knew it was impossible. He must be a kindhearted man, but tension built in her chest as she envisioned the rope hanging, mere inches away. *My God, I need your help.* Calm peace washed over her again.

"Aye, if she is willing, I can prove it."

He wouldn't give up easily. Gratitude swelled in Lia's heart toward this stranger. If only she could see who was speaking.

"Bring her to my abode," Sheriff Feroci said, his voice sounding strained. A horse moved, apparently bringing the sheriff with it.

Barat released something like a growl and the hood was slipped from her head.

"Don't untie her."

Lia looked from Barat to Dumphey, who was casting away the hood.

The soldiers half-dragged her down the street. Her whole body was numb as her mind raced forward. *If this is Lord Kiralyn and if he is my father…* How could she discern what was true between Bioti's story and this man? *Why is he only now coming to see me? If he truly is my father, why was I in Bioti's care all of these years? Did he know this?* Her breath came in short intervals as she was brought into the sheriff's home. Sheriff Feroci was now on a chair that overlooked the room, surrounded by guards.

"Now, state your cause."

Lia looked at the man who stepped forward, his focus not on the sheriff, but on her. He was dressed as a commoner. No wonder Sheriff Feroci doubted his lordship. As their gaze met, Lia's breath caught. This was the same man she had run into days before. He was Lord Kiralyn? Did he know who she was when they collided?

"Lass, I saw you limping."

Lia expected heat to flame through her cheeks. Instead, she only felt a tinge of warmth. "Aye."

"Have you a club foot?"

Not just an injury, not just a limp, but specifically a club foot? Lia's pulse quickened. "Aye."

"Of course she would claim she did if it would save her life!" Sheriff Feroci stomped his foot, causing Barat to take a step toward her.

Lord Kiralyn looked to the sheriff, a hint of amusement touching his features. "Aye, she could claim it. But I'm asking her to prove it."

Prove it? The heat that hadn't flushed her face earlier now flooded her cheeks, making her head pound. Yet if it saved her life…

"I know not how it would look now." Grief seemed to flash through Lord Kiralyn's eyes as he looked at her. "When you were born, it was sideways. The physician said it would get worse with time." He turned to talk to Sheriff Feroci again. "A plague struck my castle while I was away in battle. I was welcomed home by two graves—those of my wife and young daughter. I only recently discovered that two servants conspired together to take away my daughter—Bioti and Nes."

Lia's mouth went dry. Did this mean, then, that Bioti was never married to her father? Tears blurred her vision. He sounded so confident that she was the same lass. But how would she know that he was her father? How did he know that she was his daughter? She blinked the tears away. She wouldn't cry in the audience of the sheriff.

"Your story does not sway me," Feroci said.

Lord Kiralyn's eyes narrowed. "'T'wasn't my aim. I am asking her of her limp."

"Anyone could feign one."

"Nay. You saw her limp. The townspeople know she limps." He turned back to Lia. "May we see?"

Chapter Twenty-One

Abtshire

Raoul held his breath. He felt strangely confident, yet there was the slightest possibility he had misjudged, in which case Feroci would dub him a liar, and mayhap desire to hang him as well as the lass.

He waited while the lass—Ellia, he was certain of it—hesitated before lifting her skirt. Her face was bathed in red as she slipped her foot into sight. Though she held it in front of her, it twisted completely sideways. No child could feign that.

"How old are you, lass?"

Ellia brought her blue eyes up to meet his. They were as clear as the sky out of doors. "I am told to be thirteen."

Another piece slipping together. "Lass, do you know a madam by the name of Bioti?"

Her eyes flashed, darkening the blue as if a storm was brewing. "Aye." She almost hissed the word out. "She told me that my father died after she married him." Testing him.

"Bioti was your nursemaid. I know not why she took you away."

Someone stomped their foot. Raoul snapped his gaze to Feroci.

"Can you take your lovely chat elsewhere?" Feroci made the appearance of boredom, but Raoul detected something under the surface. And he would drive that something to full-hearted fear.

"Aye, we will. But you can rest assured that I will tell the king of your doings. He is my blood relation and will believe my every word, even if you send a warning to save yourself."

Yes, that put the fear where it belonged. Raoul turned to Ellia and offered his arm. She slipped her hand onto his elbow but kept her distance as she limped beside him.

Once outside, he turned to her as they walked. The blonde hair of the child he remembered had darkened to a golden brown. Her face had thinned with years of hardship. Yet his heart squeezed within him. She was his daughter.

"I must take you home. There is nowhere else for you to be safe."

"What is my name?"

The request made Raoul stop. "Your name?"

"Aye. You have not called me by name."

Raoul whispered the name. "Ellia."

She tilted her head to the side. "Lia," she said. "That is what Bioti called me. 'Tis close enough. Please, sir—m'lord—may I speak with my friends?"

"Noel?"

"And Dumphey, aye."

Raoul led Lia away from the crowd. Jolin stood in the distance with the two lads who had helped Lia earlier by his side.

"Lia, is he really your father?" Noel lunged toward her, wrapping his arms around her. Meanwhile, the older one—Dumphey, Raoul supposed—gave Raoul a scrutinizing look.

"I can prove I am Lord Kiralyn." Raoul started to reveal his signet.

"I need no proof," Dumphey said. His gaze went from Raoul to Ellia. "You look like father and daughter."

"We do?" Ellia's hand flew to her cheek as if desiring to see herself in comparison. She looked up shyly at Raoul, hesitant around him. Hopefully that would change with time.

"If we had only known…" Dumphey's voice trailed off and his face filled with outrage.

"I knew Bioti couldn't be your mother," Noel said.

"*Step*-mother," Ellia blurted, as if out of habit. Her eyes turned up to Raoul, full of questions. "But she wasn't truly that either, was she? She was…*my* servant?"

The way she spoke moved Raoul's heart like a rock unsettling calm water.

Dumphey's eyes hardened as he stood tall. "M'lord, I offer my assistance to find this woman."

Raoul flicked a look to Jolin, who nodded in approval. "We will be certain to send word for you." Raoul looked down at Ellia and couldn't hold back his smile. "I should like to take my daughter home before the day is passed." *My daughter.* He had never thought he'd use the words again.

He stepped back toward Jolin as Ellia lowered her voice to talk with the lads. The sorrow on her face was genuine. She didn't have to tell Raoul that she had been at least partially cared for while under Bioti's care. They wouldn't go unpaid.

When Ellia turned back to him, he held out his arm to her. He was more than ready to lead her back to the castle—to her new life.

Chapter Twenty-Two

Kiralyn Castle

Lia looked around the large nursery, taking time to observe every object.

"Do you remember anything in here?" Lord Kiralyn spoke from behind her. Lady Kiralyn must have told him where to find her.

She shook her head. "Nay…yet you say Bioti raised… your daughter here, before she disappeared?" It wasn't easy to change what she had believed all her life, as much as she desired to claim him as her father.

"Aye." Lord Kiralyn reached an arm out to the open room. "Look around to your heart's desire. I do not mind."

"Even if—" Lia stopped, her cheeks burning.

"Even if what, lass?"

Lia turned to look fully at Lord Kiralyn. His blue eyes were soft and considerate. He had shown her nothing but kindness in the few days that she had been here. "Even if I am not ready to claim these as my own? Does that disappoint you?"

The softness in Lord Kiralyn's face softened even more, if such were possible. "Ellia…" She loved his rich, baritone voice as he said her name. "You are my daughter. I desire for you to feel as if this is your home, but I understand it may take you weeks—years, even. That will never disappoint me."

The carpet was soft under Lia's bare feet as she walked forward, looking at the treasures this room had hidden for a decade. Any memory of them must be locked away in those years passed.

"Do you desire to be alone?"

Lia shook her head. "Nay. I just…" She took a shuddering breath, unable to finish her thoughts.

Lord Kiralyn walked past Lia and stopped before the bassinet. Reaching into it, he pulled out something white. "I would like you to look at this."

Lia hobbled forward. When Lord Kiralyn held out the item, she took it in her hand. Soft cloth was sewn together to make a perfect, tiny shoe.

"This is the other one." Lord Kiralyn reached into his pocket and held up another piece of white.

Lia compared it to the one she held in her hand.

Instead of being perfectly shaped, it was twisted, but the stitches were still neatly done. Someone had twisted it on purpose. "It looks as if the seamstress made a mistake."

"The seamstress made no mistake," Lord Kiralyn said. "Just like our God made no mistake when He formed you with a club foot."

Tears pricked Lia's eyes. "Fearfully and wonderfully made," she murmured. She still wasn't sure she could embrace the words Zuzene had shared with her.

Lord Kiralyn fingered the deformed shoe. "The seamstress made it to fit our babe's foot. The physicians had suggested that, with time, we could correct the foot to walk correctly. But we didn't have much of a chance to try."

The familiar heat slipped into Lia's cheeks, though Lord Kiralyn spoke of her deformity with ease and acceptance.

"Now," Lord Kiralyn continued, "I am grateful."

"Grateful?" The years of pain and humiliation were too fresh for her to be grateful for her deformity.

"Aye." Lord Kiralyn opened his hands. Lia set the little slippers on his palms. He studied them, his fingers caressing the lace sewn into the top as a smile graced his lips. "It was by your limp that I knew who you were."

Lia's heart seemed to skip a beat. If she hadn't a limp, she would be dead now.

"Even in this, God made something good come out of

what everyone would look at as a curse." He smiled at Lia as he placed the slippers back in her hands. "I would like for you to keep these."

Lia smiled as she looked down at them. Mayhap she was beginning to see how God made everything—even her limp—beautiful in His time.

Chapter Twenty-Three

Kiralyn Castle

The slippers looked right, cradled in Ellia's hands. Raoul sighed as he looked at her—his daughter. The dust and cobwebs from the dungeon were washed off her, and Elayne's hand had fitted her hair and dressed her as a princess. The blush on her cheeks had faded, and she seemed thoughtful. She was beautiful.

"M'lord."

Raoul turned as Jolin walked into the room. His shoulders stiffened. Not now. He didn't wish anything to interrupt his time with his daughter.

"They have found her." Jolin's deep voice lowered in volume. "She and her daughters await your presence in the parlor."

Ellia's spine straightened and her fingers clenched around the slippers before she seemed to realize she was crushing them.

"Thank you, Jolin." Raoul forced his voice to steady as he took Ellia's hand and placed it on his arm before leading her to follow Jolin.

"M'lord," Ellia whispered, stopping and pulling at his arm.

Raoul's heart cinched. She needn't address him so formally. He prayed the day would soon come when she would adopt the word 'Father.' He looked down as she seemed to wait for him. "What is it?"

"What if…she denies that she's ever seen me?"

Raoul shook his head. "She could attempt that, but there are too many witnesses in Abtshire who have seen you under her…" He let his voice fade before the word "care" slipped out. From what he had observed, Bioti's only concern was for herself.

When they reached the parlor door, he paused. "Shall we go in together, or should I go first?"

Ellia's body jerked in a shiver, but she lifted her chin. "I would like to go in with you."

The words threaded their way directly to his heart. *Together.* Finally, as it should be. "As you wish." He nodded to Jolin, who placed his hand on the door handle.

Ellia's grip on his arm tightened as they entered the room. He placed a hand over hers, willing her to feel assurance. Instead, he felt her cower behind him. He looked past Jolin and saw Bioti glaring at Ellia. Geva and Helga were behind Bioti, their eyes wide as they looked around them—from curiosity or fright, he couldn't tell.

He cleared his throat, but before he could speak, Bioti said, "I imagine she has filled your head with all sorts of lies."

"On the contrary, I was more interested in hearing what you had to say." Raoul's voice came out even and cool, exactly how he intended.

"M'lord." Bioti bowed before him then kept her head down. "I had heard you were killed in battle. I was afraid the enemy would come and steal away your precious daughter. So I took her to shelter her."

"Stop fabricating your story." Something inside Raoul snapped. He took a steadying breath. It would not do to lash out in anger. "You feigned Ellia's death so that you could steal her away. I don't need a long story. I would simply like to know why. Had I mistreated you? What evil had my wife or I done to you?"

As he spoke, Bioti's head lifted until she looked brazenly at him. "You don't deserve answers. Born and raised with prestige while the rest of us had to work day and night to stay alive. Born to give orders even if it meant the death of…" Here, she stopped.

Raoul looked at her, puzzled as his mind retraced the years. Gradual understanding filled him. Bioti's husband had died working the fields. She blamed him?

"What about Nes, then? Why did you kill him?"

Bioti's steel-gray eyes filled with satisfaction. "You had better ask your man about Nes's death."

His man? What man? Raoul turned to look at Jolin, whose brow had the same knitted look as a few days before—when they were discussing Galien. Raoul took a staggering breath.

"That will be enough, Bioti." He turned to Jolin. "You may assist these three."

Bioti cast a hard look his way, her lips pressed into a thin line.

As Jolin passed by Raoul, he leaned in. "A word with you, m'lord."

The gravity of his voice cut off Raoul's breath altogether. He motioned for another servant to take Bioti.

When the door shut, Raoul slicked his hair back with his hands. Beside him, Ellia squirmed and stepped toward the door.

"You may stay." This would involve her as much as it did him. He sank down onto the settee and motioned for Ellia to sit beside him. The comfort he felt, having his daughter by his side, did nothing to appease the anxiety building in his chest. "What is this all about?"

Ellia shrank away from him, as if fearing that Jolin's words would give her an unwanted blow. Raoul laid his hand gently over her work-worn fingers and turned his eyes to Jolin, demanding an answer.

Jolin paced the room in front of them. "I have taken the liberty to secure Galien and question him."

"Whatever for? What did he do?" Raoul didn't want to hear the answers. His mind had already calculated the many times that Galien was absent during their search, with never a report to account for his actions. He didn't want to put the pieces together.

Jolin took a deep breath. "I wish I didn't have to bring bad news on top of your happy reunion…"

"Out with it, man. I need to know every detail."

Jolin frowned and rubbed his face, the very action seeming to intensify the tension in Raoul's shoulders. "Galien is angry with you, m'lord. I have suspected his irritation with you in years past, but I thought he had gotten over it." He sat down and rested his hands on his knees, leaning forward in confidence, no longer a servant, but the friend he had come to be.

"He has been my faithful servant—companion—for over a decade. Have I done anything to cause this anger? How have I wronged him?" Raoul's heart sent up a prayer as he spoke. *Father, I have tried to live pleasing Thee in dealing with those under me. If this is my wrong, forgive me, and give me wisdom in what to do.*

"When we were off in battle during the plague, his daughter died. Galien's mother was a healer, and she taught him well."

"Aye, which is why I took Galien with me," Raoul said. Jolin still hadn't answered his questions.

"He blamed you for the death of his child. Had he been here, and not with you, he is convinced that he could have found the correct herbs and saved her life. He appeased his wrath, because your daughter also died. Now that she was discovered alive…" Jolin looked toward Ellia.

It wasn't possible. Raoul massaged his forehead as his mind scrambled back over the past few years. Galien had accepted the death of his daughter, just as he himself had been forced to accept the death of Ellia.

"Galien changed…the day the news of Ellia arrived." Jolin stood up again and began walking back and forth. "He had found Nes and talked with him when we went to Fordyce the first time. I had no reason to doubt his report."

"Yet he led us astray, to Matheny?"

"Aye. He knew Ellia was in Abtshire the entire time."

Raoul sank further into the cushions of the settee. "Galien never wanted me to find her." He whispered the words, trying to make himself angry at the man. Instead, intense pity filled him. "He wanted her to stay dead to me—like his daughter shall always be to him."

Jolin stopped his pacing and laid steadying hands on Raoul's shoulders. "He claims that Nes's death was an accident. Nes was old and frail, already nigh death." He gave a low sigh. "I fear Galien took his pent-up wrath out on Nes."

There were no words to reply to that. Raoul clenched his fists and released them slowly. Betrayed, by a man he trusted with his life.

"I shall make arrangements for him to be heard at the king's court."

Raoul nodded numbly. Fordyce was in Lord Trent's domain. 'Twould be easier to settle with the king overseeing the matter. He looked up to meet Jolin's gaze. "I shall leave that in your hands."

Jolin nodded, bowed, then left the room.

Chapter Twenty-Four

Kiralyn Castle

It was her fault. Of course it was. Lia looked down at the dark wood that lined the floor and tried to stop her knees from shaking. She felt Lord Kiralyn's hand on her arm, but didn't look up. He was trying to assure her, she knew, but she couldn't swallow the lump that formed in her throat.

Lord Kiralyn placed a finger on Lia's chin and brought her face up to look at him.

"You needn't worry, Ellia."

Lia shook her head and blinked back tears. "But 'tis my fault." Her voice caught as she said the words, fear knotting her stomach.

Lord Kiralyn shook his head, his face sober. "Do not blame yourself. Galien made his own choices, regardless of his reasoning behind them." He took a deep, shuddering breath. "We shall move forward from here." He stood and held out his arm to Lia.

Lia looked at Lord Kiralyn's kind smile and placed her hand on his arm. She stood to her feet and steadied herself.

As they walked down the hall, Lia asked, "What of Bioti and her daughters?" If Bioti had been arrested even a week ago, she would have been ecstatic with joy. Something had changed inside, though. She was grateful that Bioti no longer would get away with her wiles, but pity for the daughters filled her.

"There will be trial," Lord Kiralyn said, his tone soft and gentle, as if he was figuring out how to say the words without causing her to be upset. "Bioti will likely be found guilty of many things—both against me, and against Lord Feroci."

"But she won't be…hanged? Will she?" Lia's near-death experience caused a shudder to vibrate her body. Nay, she wouldn't wish that upon anyone—even Bioti.

"Seeing as she is legally my servant, I do have a say in that matter." Lord Kiralyn stopped and turned to face her, his gentle blue eyes looking at her seriously. "And if it would disturb you for such to be her demise…mayhap a lifetime in the gaol would be wise?"

The tension in Lia's shoulders eased slightly and she found herself nodding. "What of Geva and Helga? They were but her daughters—and though they were cruel at times, I cannot help but lay blame to Bioti."

"Aye." Lord Kiralyn nodded. "We will explore other options for them. Mayhap place them in a family whose care will lead them in the right direction?"

Now, Lia smiled. "That would be gracious."

Lord Kiralyn patted her hand as he led her into another parlor where Lady Kiralyn sat, needle and thread in hand. One day, Lia hoped she would be able to keep straight the numerous rooms in this castle.

Lady Kiralyn stood, laying aside her fancy work. "Ellia…" She reached out and gathered Lia's rough, calloused hands in her own.

Lia loved hearing the gentleness with which Lord and Lady Kiralyn said her new name. She would be more than happy to replace the "Lia" that Bioti used in her harsh tones.

"I see we shall have to set up a schedule of sorts so that you may be shared equally with both Raoul and me." Lady Kiralyn's eyes were filled with love as she looked from her husband to Lia.

Lia allowed herself to be led to the settee and nestled between the two of them—Lord Kiralyn lounging back, seeming relaxed and satisfied, Lady Kiralyn sitting neatly on the edge, proper and precise.

"Ellia." Lord Kiralyn shifted, as if to see Lia better. "I realize that Elayne is not your mother by birth, and that you barely know me as your father…but we would be honored if you decide that you can call us 'Mother' and

'Father.'" He reached down and squeezed her hand. "It may take years. We're willing to wait."

"Mother. Father." The names rolled deliciously off her tongue and she kept her tears at bay. How many times had she hidden away, whispering them where no one could hear, longing for someone to be such to her? She looked up at Lord Kiralyn. "I think I am ready to use them very soon, m'lord—Father." She was ready—more than ready—to embrace the changes offered her. She looked from Lord to Lady Kiralyn…Father and Mother. Smiles broadened on their faces and tears glistened in Mother's eyes.

Father lowered his head and planted a kiss on Lia's golden brown hair. "I should like that, Ellia, very much."

Discussion Questions

1) How did Bioti's and Nes's choices affect the lives of others? Have you thought much about the choices that you make and how they affect others?
2) What was Raoul's initial struggle? How did his struggle intensify throughout the story?
3) How did he learn to overcome this struggle? What choices could he have made sooner?
4) What lessons did Raoul learn that you could apply to your own life? Are there areas in which you're afraid to trust God? Do you have pieces of your heart that you're scared to surrender to Him?
5) What is one verse that you turn to when you are struggling?
6) How would you react if you were Lia, under Bioti's guardianship?
7) How could Lia be made beautiful, even though she suffered from a deformity which, in her lifetime, would never be healed?

8) Do you struggle with accepting the way that God made you—flaws and all? Are you learning, like Lia, to embrace the way God shaped you?
9) Have you, like Lia, experienced the beautiful gift of salvation—the healing of the deformity of your soul?
10) Even if you have never been given the opportunity of a "fresh start" like Lia, has there been any point at which your life changed? How did God use those moments in your life?

Historical Note

The *Tales of Faith* series is what I consider my "fantasy" medieval series. Fantasy in that I am not specifically basing it in a certain era or country. The lands, castles, and characters in *Tales of Faith* are completely from my imagination. While I have gleaned some historical tidbits from the medieval era, I am not writing this as a historical fiction series. Thus, some things may hint at modern for the time.

Author's Note

It is all the fault of my author-friend, A.M. Heath. Not long after "Befriending the Beast" released, she messaged me, "Have you ever thought of doing a Cinderella story, where the prince is the father?" I stayed up until midnight with my mind churning the what-ifs. I think I got the title before I really solidified an idea. "The Secret Slipper" has had many firsts for me: writing from two perspectives, writing as a married character, and having an active antagonist to mention a few. I have not enjoyed every moment of writing, re-writing, editing, and learning, but looking back, it is something I wouldn't want to trade, for I have learned so much!

Now for thanks…these are getting harder and harder to write, as there seems to be so many who offer their assistance.

Anita – like I said, this was your fault. ;) Thank you so much for being my writing mentor and selflessly offering your brain and expertise to help me! My writing has grown from your friendship.

Faith – you've been my accountability writing partner for the process of this story. You've helped me to stay on my toes, and I'm grateful!

Kenzi – how many times have you read my manuscript? Just as many times as I have, I do believe. I don't think you know just how much I appreciate your prayers, encouragement, and suggestions with my many projects.

Elizabeth (SunKissed Photography) – the picture of Lia! I am so honored to use your photography for my book cover, and grateful for you allowing me to use it (and thanks to Rachel W., the subject).

Mom – the years of red pen seem to have finally paid off! Thank you for your unending encouragement in my writing.

My Family – thanks for bearing with me as I talked about my characters and ideas and everything. Your support means so much!

My FaceBook Street Team – thanks for letting me flood your newsfeed on my writing days with questions, thoughts, and prayer requests! Y'all are an amazing support!

To those who read my pathetic and very needy first-draft: Katie, Janell, Rachel, Anita, Kenzi, and Aimee. Thanks for your suggestions and input. You always make me think twice as I edit, and I need that! Special thanks to Katie and Rachel, who also read this manuscript multiple times. Y'all are amazing!

My beta-readers: Faith, Olivia, Jesseca, Kellyn, Hannah,

AnneMarie, Liberty Baehr, Liberty Bluebelle, Alicia, Marlene, Darcy, Hanna, Esther, Joanna, Naomi, Emily...your help was wonderful! I know that this Slipper shines because of your input!

Again, my heart is overflowing with gratitude to my Lord Jesus Christ. Not only does He supply ideas for new stories, He is also faithful to give me wisdom for every place I have questions. To Him belongs all glory and honor, for without Him, I am nothing.

And to you, my reader, *thank you.* Unless you are also an author, you likely do not know how encouraging it is for me to have you reading my book and leaving your reviews! Thank you.

Until next time,

Amanda Tero

Connect with Amanda

Email: amandaterobooks@gmail.com
Website: www.amandatero.com
Facebook: www.facebook.com/amandaterobooks
Instagram: amandateroauthor
Pinterest: amandaruthtero
Blog: www.withajoyfulnoise.blogspot.com
Goodreads: AmandaTero

Other stories by Amanda Tero

Journey to Love

(an Orphan Journeys novella)

Now orphaned, Marie is swept miles away from the only life she knew to be sheltered by unknown guardians. Caught in the challenges of a new life, she cannot prevent changes from happening, but she can keep the Bowles and their friends at arm's length. Or can she?

While things appear to transition smoothly on the outside, Marie struggles against the turmoil she faces on the inside. She sees something in the Bowles and her new friends that she had never experienced before...but should she trust what the preacher is teaching when it goes against everything she had accepted as truth? Is God really a God of love? If He is, then is Marie willing to accept it?

Follow Marie as she begins the journey to love.

Letter of Love

(Short story sequel to Journey to Love,
Can be read as a stand-alone)

Edward Dixon is convinced that life is cruel, and he is not willing for anything to change his mind from that. A letter from his sister, Marie, reveals that she views life otherwise. Will her letter, filled with love and forgiveness, make a difference in Edward's life? Or will he stubbornly refuse to change before it's too late?

Befriending the Beast

(Tales of Faith – Book 1)

Belle has returned unannounced to the castle to restore her relationship with the king, her father. Her hopes are dashed with the devastating message: "The king refuses to see you." Convinced that God has led her home, she is unwilling to return to Lord and Lady Kiralyn.

Time is running out for the decision that will change her life. When tragedy strikes, will she and her father be pulled further apart or knit together? Could she stay at the castle even if she will never see her father again?

Short Stories

Coffee Cake Days

Meg has finally graduated and has the time she's dreamed of for months: time to "sit at the feet of Jesus" and soak up His Word as she seeks what future plans He has for her. She soon runs into a problem: her family.

Unwanted interruptions and household duties tear her away from the time she longs to spend in the Bible. Journey with her as she strives to learn the balance of spending time in God's Word and applying it to her daily life.

Debt of Mercy

Raboc's eyes narrowed to slits and he thrust his arm forward until his fingers closed around Ancel's throat. The young man knew better than to resist the powerful lord, but his jaw clenched.

"To the dungeon with you. Guards!"

"Lord, have mercy," Ancel pleaded. "Give me time and I shall pay the other half."

A medieval retelling of the parable in Matthew 18

Hartly Manor

There were six of them…

And these six children have an important lesson to learn when it comes to Mr. Hartly and his manor. Is he the scary man that Rees says he is? Or will the children discover something else as they get to know him?

Letters from a Scatter-Brained Sister

"How could you, in good conscience, leave the kitchen in the hands of me, a giddy sixteen-year-old??"

So begins Nicole's letters to her sister who has recently "deserted" the family because of marriage. As Nicole attempts to take over the kitchen, she begins to wonder if the kitchen will take over her?

Maggie's Hope Chest

It was the gift that Maggie had desired throughout her teen years.

Yet was God's purpose for this gift for her to fulfill her own desires? Or did He have something much better in store? Something that Maggie could not quite understand?

Noelle's Gift

Mama needed happiness for Christmas, but Noelle was only eight. What gift could she give?

Peace, Be Still

Twelve-year-old Keith is left in charge of the lighthouse and his two younger siblings while his dad goes out in the storm to help a ship in distress. As the long night passes with waves pounding against the lighthouse, fear threatens to engulf him.

Can Keith stay awake and keep the lights burning? Will he worry away the night, or will he find comfort and peace in trusting God's promises?

Have you met the Master Author?

The "author and finisher of our faith," the "author of salvation?"

Well, why do we need to know the Master Author?

There is no man, woman, boy, or girl who is without sin. Romans 3:23 says, "For **all** have sinned, and come short of the glory of God;"

Have you lied, cheated, stolen, taken God's Name in vain, coveted, or lusted? All of these are sins according to God's Holy law (see Exodus 20). Even if we neglect in just one area of God's law, we are found sinners. "For whosoever shall keep the whole law, and yet offend in one point, he is guilty of all." (James 2:10) The payment for sin is death ("For the wages of sin is death;" Romans 6:23a)

God does not desire to leave us in this hopeless, destitute state. He did what we could not do and paid the debt for us. He sent His Son, Jesus Christ, to come, be born of a virgin, live a sinless, perfect life, die a cruel death, and rise again, victorious over sin, death, and hell! Romans 6:23 continues to say, "but the gift of God is eternal life through Jesus Christ our Lord." Jesus Christ is the only way to have eternal life, to be forgiven ("Jesus saith unto him, I am the way, the truth, and the life: no man cometh unto the Father, but by me.” John 14:6). God promised us that, "If we confess our sins, He is faithful and just to forgive us our sins, and to cleanse us from all unrighteousness.” (1 John 1:9)

Salvation comes by putting your faith and trust in Jesus Christ for salvation and eternity ("Believe on the Lord Jesus Christ, and thou shalt be saved, ” Acts 16:31) and repenting from our sins ("Repent ye therefore, and be converted, that your sins may be blotted out,” Acts 3:19).

So, have you met the Author?

www.ingramcontent.com/pod-product-compliance
Lightning Source LLC
Chambersburg PA
CBHW061240170626
46809CB00007B/2755

* 9 7 8 1 9 4 2 9 3 1 2 3 2 *